英文精短美文激情诵读

The Moving Heart

感动心灵

段颖立 雷涛 等 编著

中国水利水电出版社
www.waterpub.com.cn

内 容 提 要

本书精选了 60 余篇脍炙人口的英文精短美文，分为爱情篇、友情篇、亲情篇和欣赏篇四部分，采用英汉对照的方式安排内容，便于读者阅读学习，是不可多得的阅读、学习和收藏精品。

本书适用于不同层次的英语爱好者学习和休闲阅读。

图书在版编目（CIP）数据

感动心灵：英汉对照/段颖立等编著. —北京：中国水
利水电出版社，2007
（英文精短美文激情诵读）
ISBN 978 - 7 - 5084 - 4845 - 9

Ⅰ.感… Ⅱ.段… Ⅲ.①英语—汉语—对照读物②散文—
作品集—世界 Ⅳ.H319.4:I

中国版本图书馆 CIP 数据核字（2007）第 108415 号

书　　　名	英文精短美文激情诵读 **感动心灵**
作　　　者	段颖立　雷涛　等　编著
出 版 发 行	中国水利水电出版社（北京市三里河路6号　100044） 网址：www. waterpub. com. cn E - mail：sales@ waterpub. com. cn 电话：（010）63202266（总机）、68331835（营销中心）
经　　　售	北京科水图书销售中心（零售） 电话：（010）88383994、63202643 全国各地新华书店和相关出版物销售网点
排　　　版	福瑞来书装
印　　　刷	北京市地矿印刷厂
规　　　格	710mm×1000mm　16 开本　15.75 印张　306 千字
版　　　次	2007 年 9 月第 1 版　2008 年 4 月第 2 次印刷
印　　　数	5001—8000 册
定　　　价	**28.80 元**

英文精短美文激情诵读

感动心灵

主　　编：段颖立　雷　涛

编　　者：段颖立　雷　涛　李云鹏　刘　恒
　　　　　王　月　高　洁　韩伟民　毛　晗
　　　　　赵国亚　郑崑琳　芦　涵　郭立萍
　　　　　王福强　李宇环　艾　静　陈轶斐
　　　　　郑　炎　郭　爿　郭宗炎　侯卫群

CONTENTS

爱情篇

友 情 篇

感动心灵 •••

III

亲 情 篇

欣 赏 篇

I love you not because of who you are, but because of who I am when I am with you.

我爱你不是因为你是谁，而是我在你面前是谁。

Whatever Love Means

There are many different kinds of love. Love between parents and children, between siblings, relatives, lovers, friends, and colleagues. In North America, people are very open and expressive about their feelings. Parents hug and kiss their children all the time. It is also quite common to see young couples kissing in public.

It's not surprising that many, if not all, languages have so much choice in how to express romantic feelings. Love is among the strongest of emotions, and over the centuries, so much has been written about it. It is thought that the majority of all songs ever written deal with love in one way or another!

Other than language, there is not much difference in how people express love feelings. Love is a very basic emotion, and it doesn't matter where you come from, the feelings are probably the same everywhere.

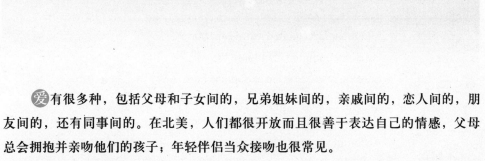

　　爱有很多种，包括父母和子女间的，兄弟姐妹间的，亲戚间的，恋人间的，朋友间的，还有同事间的。在北美，人们都很开放而且很善于表达自己的情感，父母总会拥抱并亲吻他们的孩子；年轻伴侣当众接吻也很常见。

　　大部分的语言都有无数种方式表达浪漫情感，这一点并不足为奇。爱是最强烈的情感之一。几个世纪以来，爱情故事数不胜数，而几乎所有的歌曲都这样那样的与爱情有关。

　　除了语言不同外，人们在表达情感时几乎没什么不同。爱情是最基本的情感，无论你来自何方，这种感觉都是相似的。

爱情的 见 证
Love's Witness

Slight unpremeditated Words are borne，

By every common Wind into the Air；

Carelessly uttered, die as soon as born，

And in one instant give both Hope and Fear：

Breathing all Contraries with the same Wind.

According to the Caprice of the Mind.

But Billet-doux are constant Witnesses，

Substantial Records to Eternity；

Just Evidences，who the Truth confess，

On which the Lover safely may rely；

They' re serious Thoughts，digested and resolved；

And last，when Words are into Clouds devolved.

不假思索的轻率话语，

随风消失在空中；

随便说说，刚出口即消失，

一瞬间给人希望和恐惧：

同一气息呼出万般矛盾心肠，

追随心灵无常的遐想。

但情书则是恒常的见证，

直至永恒的实体记录；

公道的证物，它道出真诚，

恋人能在其上安心依附；

它们是严肃的思想，经过深思熟虑，

当话语在云外消失，它们还将延续。

witness *v.*

目击，作证

unpremeditated *adj.*

非预谋的

utter *v.*

说出

caprice *n.*

反复无常

billet-doux *n.*

情书

confess *v.*

坦白，忏悔

resolve *v.*

决心，解决

devolve *v.*

转移，传下

Carelessly uttered, die as soon as born.

随便说说，刚出口即消失。

They're serious Thoughts, digested and resolved;

它们是严肃的思想，经过深思熟虑；

内在美 *Beauty Within*

John Blanchard stood up from the bench, straightened his army uniform, and studied the crowd of people making their way through the Grand Central Station.

He looked for the girl whose heart he knew, but whose face he didn't, the girl with the rose. His interest in her had begun 12 months before in a Florida library. Taking a book off the shelf he found himself absorbed, not by the words of the book, but by the notes penciled in the margin. The soft handwriting showed a thoughtful soul and insightful mind.

In the front of the book, he discovered the previous owner's name, Miss Hollis Maynell. With time and effort he found her exact address. She lived in New York City. He wrote her a letter introducing himself and inviting her to answer him. The next day he was shipped to another country for service in World War II.

During the next year and one month the two grew to know each other through the mail. Each letter was a seed falling on a fertile heart. A love began to develop. Blanchard requested a photograph, but she refused. She explained: "If your feeling for me has any reality, any honest basis, what I look like won't matter. Suppose I'm beautiful I'd always be worried by the feeling that you had been taking a chance on just that, and that kind of love would make me sick. Suppose I'm plain (and you must admit that this is more likely). Then I would always fear that you were going on writing to me only because you were lonely and had no one else. No, don't ask for my picture. When you come to New York, you shall see me and then you shall make your own decision. Remember, both of us are free to stop or to go on after that—whichever we choose..."

约翰·布兰查德从长凳上站起身来，整了整军装，留意着格兰德中央车站进出的人群。

他在寻找一位姑娘，一位佩带玫瑰的姑娘，一位他只知其心，不知其貌的姑娘。12个月前，在佛罗里达州的一个图书馆，他对她产生了兴趣。他从书架上取下一本书，很快便被吸引住了，不是被书的内容，而是被空白处铅笔写的批语所吸引。柔和的笔迹显示出其人多思善虑的心灵和富有洞察力的头脑。

在书的前页，他找到了书的前任主人的姓名：霍利斯·梅奈尔小姐。他花了一番工夫，找到了她的确切地址，她住在纽约市。他给她写了一封信介绍自己，并请她回复。第二天他被运送到海外，参加第二次世界大战。

在接下来的一年零一个月中，两人通过信件来往增进了对彼此的了解。每一封信都如一颗种子撒入肥沃的心灵之土，浪漫的爱情之花就要绽开。布兰查德提出要一张照片，可她拒绝了。她解释道："如果你对我的感情是真实的，是诚心诚意的，那我的容貌如何并不重要。设想我美丽动人，我会始终深感不安，惟恐你只是因为我的容貌就贸然与我相爱，而这种爱情令我厌恶。设想本人相貌平平（你得承认，这种可能性更大），那我就会始终担心，你和我保持通信仅仅是出于孤独寂寞，无人交谈。不，别索要照片。等你到了纽约，你会见到我，到时你可再作定夺。切记，见面后我俩都可以自由决定中止关系或继续交往——无论你我怎么选择……"

uniform *n.*

制服

absorb *v.*

吸收，吸引

margin *n.*

页边的空白

thoughtful *adj.*

深思的，有思想的

insightful *adj.*

富有洞察力的，有见解的

fertile *adj.*

肥沃的，富饶的

plain *adj.*

平常的，一般的；朴素的

Taking a book off the shelf he found himself absorbed, not by the words of the book, but by the notes penciled in the margin.

他从书架上取下一本书，很快便被吸引住了，不是被书的内容，而是被空白处铅笔写的批语所吸引。

Each letter was a seed falling on a fertile heart.

每一封信都如一颗种子撒入肥沃的心灵之土。

Suppose I'm beautiful I'd always be worried by the feeling that you had been taking a chance on just that, and that kind of love would make me sick.

设想我美丽动人，我会始终深感不安，惟恐你只是因为我的容貌就贸然与我相爱，而这种爱情令我厌恶。

时光流逝
As Time Goes by

Progress in predicting the outcome of relationships, and information about the genetic roots of fidelity, might also make proposing marriage more like a job application — with associated medical, genetic and psychological checks. If it were reliable enough, would insurers cover you for divorce? And as brain scanners become cheaper and more widely available, they might go from being research tools to something that anyone could use to find out how well they were loved. Will the future bring answers to questions such as: Does your partner really love you? Is your husband lusting after the student of study abroad working for your family?

And then there are drugs. Despite Dr·Fisher's reservations, might they also help people to fall in love, or perhaps fix broken relationships? Probably not. Dr·Pfaus says that drugs may enhance portions of the "love experience" but fall short of doing the whole job because of their specificity. And if a couple fall out of love, drugs are unlikely to help either. Dr·Fisher does not believe that the brain could overlook distaste for someone — even if a couple in troubles could inject themselves with huge amounts of dopamine.

However, she does think that administering serotonin can help someone get over a bad love affair faster. She also suggests it is possible to trick the brain into feeling romantic love in a long-term relationship by doing novel things with your partner. Any arousing activity drives up the level of dopamine and can therefore trigger feelings of romance as a side effect. This is why holidays can rekindle passion. Romantics, of course, have always known that love is a special sort of chemistry. Scientists are now beginning to show how true this is.

通过彼此关联的医学、遗传基因和心理学的检查，预测人际关系最终结果的研究进展和关于忠诚度的遗传基础信息，能使求婚变得更像工作申请。如果这个结论足够可信，保险公司会为你的婚姻投保吗？当脑扫描仪变得更便宜更普及时，它能由研究工具变成任何人都可以用于发现他们被爱到何种程度的手段吗？未来会不会就如下问题为人类找到答案：你的伴侣是否真的爱你？你的丈夫是否正对来家打工的留学女生暗送秋波？

接下来当然会有相应的药物。但是Fisher博士对此有所保留：药物是否可能帮助人们坠入爱河，或者稳固破裂的关系？或许不能完全做到。对此另一位学者Pfaus博士如是说：药物可能部分地提高"恋爱体验"，但因为其特殊性，达不到整体提高的效果。如果一对夫妇不再相爱，药物多半无能为力。Fisher博士不相信大脑可以忽略对某人的厌恶——即使对婚姻危机中的夫妇大量注射了多巴胺，也于事无补。

然而，她确实认为调控血液复合胺水平能更快地帮助人走出恋爱的低谷。她同时建议和你的伴侣做一些新鲜事，这样可能哄骗大脑在长期两性关系中依然能感觉到爱情的甜美。任何唤醒活动都会提高多巴胺的水平而引发浪漫的感受。这就是为什么假日能重新点燃激情的原因所在。当然，爱情浪漫主义者总是认为爱情是一种特殊的化学，而正是科学家们，现在开始展示出了这一看法是如何的千真万确。

genetic *adj.*

遗传的，起源的

fidelity *n.*

忠实

propose *v.*

求婚

psychological *adj.*

心理上的

cover *v.*

担保

specificity *n.*

特异性

dopamine *n.*

多巴胺(一种治脑神经病的药物)

serotonin *n.*

含于血液中的复合胺

trigger *v.*

引发，触发

rekindle *v.*

重新点燃

And as brain scanners become cheaper and more widely available, they might go from being research tools to something that anyone could use to find out how well they were loved.

当脑扫描仪变得更便宜更普及时，它能由研究工具变成任何人都可以用于发现他们被爱到何种程度的手段吗？

Dr·Pfaus says that drugs may enhance portions of the "love experience" but fall short of doing the whole job because of their specificity.

对此另一位学者Pfaus博士如是说：药物可能部分地提高"恋爱体验"，但因为其特殊性，达不到整体提高的效果。

However, she does think that administering serotonin can help someone get over a bad love affair faster.

然而，她确实认为调控血液复合胺水平能更快地帮助人走出恋爱的低谷。

Any arousing activity drives up the level of dopamine and can therefore trigger feelings of romance as a side effect.

任何唤醒活动都会提高多巴胺的水平而引发浪漫的感受。

爱的故事 A Love Story

Once upon a time, there was an island where all the feelings lived: Happiness, Sadness, Richness, Vanity and Love. One day it was announced that the island would sink, so all repaired their boats and left.

Love wanted to persevere until the last possible moment. When the island was almost sinking, Love decided to ask for help. Richness was passing by Love in a grand boat. Love said, "Richness, can you take me with you?" Richness answered, "No, I can't. There is a lot of gold and silver in my boat. There is no place here for you."

Love decided to ask Vanity who was also passing by in a beautiful vessel, "Vanity, please help me!" "I can't help you, Love. You are all wet and might damage my boat." Vanity answered.

Sadness was close by so Love asked for help, Sadness, let me go with you. "Oh...Love, I am so sad that I need to be by myself!"

Happiness passed by Love too, but she was so happy that she did not even hear when Love called her!

Suddenly, there was a voice, "Come Love, I will take you." It was an elder. Love felt so blessed and overjoyed that he even forgot to ask the elder his name. When they arrived at dry land, the elder went his own way.

Realizing how much he owed the elder, Love and asked Knowledge, another elder, "Who helped me?" "It was Time," Knowledge answered. "Time?" asked Love. "But why did Time help me?" Knowledge smiled with deep wisdom and answered, "Because, only Time is capable of understanding how great Love is."

从前有一个岛，所有的感情都住在那里：幸福、悲伤、富有、虚荣和爱。一天，听说小岛即将沉没，因此所有的情感都准备小船，纷纷离开。

爱希望能坚持到最后一刻。小岛即将沉没了，爱决定请求帮助。富有驾者一艘大船从爱身边经过，爱说："富有，你能带上我么？"富有回答说："不行，我的船上载满金银财宝，没有你的地方。"

虚荣坐在漂亮的小船中从爱身边驶过，爱问："虚荣，你能帮助我吗？"虚荣说："不行，你全身湿透，会弄脏我的船的。"

悲伤的船靠近了，爱问："悲伤，请带我走吧。""哦……爱，我太难过了，想一个人呆着。"

persevere *v.*
坚持

vessel *n.*
船，容器

blessed *adj.*
赐予幸福、快乐或满足的

overjoyed *adj.*
狂喜的，极端高兴的

wisdom *n.*
智慧

幸福经过爱的身边，她太开心了，根本没听见爱在呼唤。

突然，一个声音喊道："来，爱，我带你走。" 声音来自一位老者。爱太高兴了，甚至忘了问老者的名字。当他们来到岸上，老者自己离开了。

爱突然意识到老者给了它多大的帮助，爱问另一位老者——知识："谁帮助了我？"知识说："是时间。""时间？"爱问："但是时间为什么帮助我？"知识睿智地微笑道："因为只有时间了解爱有多伟大。"

Love felt so blessed and overjoyed that he even forgot to ask the elder his name.

爱太高兴了，甚至忘了问老者的名字。

Because, only Time is capable of understanding how great Love is.

因为只有时间了解爱有多伟大。

爱 只是一根线
Love Is Just a Thread

Anonymous

佚名

Sometimes I really doubt whether there is love between my parents. Every day they are very busy trying to earn money in order to pay the high tuition for my brother and me. They don't act in the romantic ways that I read in books or I see on TV. in their opinion, "I love you"is too luxurious for them to say. Sending flowers to each other on Valentine's Day is even more out of the question. Finally my father has a bad temper. When he's very tired from the hard work，it is easy for him to lose his temper.

　　有时候，我真的怀疑父母之间是否有真爱。他们天天忙于赚钱，为我和弟弟支付学费。他们从未像我在书中读到，或在电视中看到的那样互诉衷肠。他们认为"我爱你"太奢侈，很难说出口。更不用说在情人节送花这样的事了。我父亲的脾气非常坏。经过一天的劳累之后，他特别容易发脾气。

One day， my mother was sewing a quilt. I silently sat down beside her and looked at her.

一天，母亲正在缝被子，我静静地坐在她旁边看着她。

"Mom，I have a question to ask you，" I said after a while.

过了一会儿，我说："妈妈，我想问你一个问题。"

"What？" she replied，still doing her work.

"什么问题？"她一边继续缝着，一边回答道。

"Is there love between you and Dad？"I asked her in a very low voice.

我低声地问道："你和爸爸之间有没有爱情啊？"

My mother stopped her work and raised her head with surprise in her eyes. She didn't answer immediately. Then she bowed her head and continued to sew zhe quit.

母亲突然停下了手中的活，满眼诧异地抬起头。她没有立即作答。然后低下头，继续缝被子。

I was very worried because I thought I had hurt her .I was in a great embarrassment and I didn't know what I should do. But at last I heard my mother say the following words:

我担心伤害了她。我非常尴尬，不知道该怎么办。不过，后来我听见母亲说：

"Susan，" she said thoughtfully，"Look at this thread. Sometimes it appears, but most of it disappears in the quilt. The thread really makes the quilt strong and durable. If life is a quilt, then love should be a thread. It can hardly be seen anywhere or anytime ,but it's really there. Love is inside."

"苏珊，看看这些线。有时候，你能看得见，但是大多数都隐藏在被子里。这些线使被子坚固耐用。如果生活就像一床被子，那么爱就是其中的线。你不可能随时随地看到它，但是它却实实在在地存在着。爱是内在的。"母亲若有所思地说。

I listened carefully but I couldn't understand her until the next spring. At that time, my father suddenly got sick seriously. My mother had to stay with him in the hospital for a month. When they returned from the hospital, they both looked very pale. It seemed both of them had had a serious illness.

我仔细地听着，却无法明由她的话，直到来年的春天。那时候，我父亲得了重病，母亲在医院里呆了一个月。当他们从医院回来的时候，都显得非常苍白，就像他们都得了 场重病 样。

After they were back. every day in the morning and dusk, my mother he|ped rny father walk slowly on the country road. My father had never been so gentle It seemed they were the most harmonious coupIe. Along the country road，there were many beautiful flowers. green grass and trees. The sun gently glistened through the leaves. All of these made up the most beautiful picture in the world.

他们回来之后，每天清晨或黄昏，母亲都会搀扶着父亲在乡村小路上漫步。父亲从未如此温和过，他们就像是天作之合。在小路旁边，有许多美丽的野花，绿草和树木。阳光穿过树叶的缝隙，温柔地照射在地面上。这一切形成了一幅世间最美好的画面。

The doctor had said my father would recover in two months. But after two months he still couldn't walk by himself. All of us were worried about him.

医生说父亲将在两个月后康复。但是两个月过后，他仍然无法独立行走。我们都很为他担心。

"Dad, how are you feeling now?"I asked him one day.

有一天，我问他："爸爸，你感觉怎么样？"

"Susan, don't worry about me." He said gently. "To tell you the truth. I just like walking with your mom. I like this kind of life." Reading his eyes,I know he loves my mother deeply.

他温和地说："苏珊，不用为我担心。跟你说吧，我喜欢与你妈妈一块散步的感觉。我喜欢这种生活。"从他的眼神里，我看得出他对母亲的爱之深刻。

Once I thought love meant flowers, gifts and sweet kisses. But from this experience, I understand that love is just a thread in the quilt of our life. Love is inside, making life strong and warm…

我曾经认为爱情就是鲜花、礼物和甜蜜的亲吻。但是，从那一刻起，我明白了，爱情就像生活中被子里的一根线。爱情就在里面，使生活变得坚固而温暖……

约会第一定律
The First Rule of Dating

It is 5:30 on a Friday afternoon and you have just had another long workweek. You finally get home, get something to eat, sit down on the couch with the TV remote control in one hand, and the mail in the other. Looking through the mail, you see a letter from your sweetheart. You rip open the letter and the words— "I don't think we should see each other anymore" explode off the page. This is a letter bomb, not love note! Your heart sinks into your stomach as you realize that the person who you invested so much time, energy and emotion into has disappeared and ended something that you hoped would last a lifetime. After the first shock, you check your calls, hoping there has been a mistake, a message from your sweetheart, or at least a few words to ease the blow. Nothing. You feel deeply hurt, rejected and all alone.

Months pass and you are not feeling any better. You ask yourself, what went wrong? Who's to blame? Why did such a good thing go bad? Finally, a new truth starts to emerge, and you realize why this relationship fizzled: you didn't have your own life. This person was your life; your whole self-worth was wrapped up in someone else. You see that your life was on hold – your career, your interests, your friends, were all dependant on someone else. Thus you had little to give to the relationship, and when the relationship ended you had nothing for yourself.

Sometimes when you break up with your loved one, you learn the most valuable lesson of dating—the most important thing a person can give to a relationship is their own, individual life! When you invest all your energy and self-esteem in getting a date or having a relationship, you don't have a life.

People with lives are not waiting to be swept off their feet. People with lives do not make "getting married" their ultimate life goal. People with lives do not always have to be in a relationship or on a date to feel good about their lives. People with lives are not barhopping in hopes of finding "the one." Relationships and marriage are important goals, but they must be kept in perspective. When romantic relationships are an obsession or become the most important thing in your life, you've got a problem!

Here is the sobering news: If you don't have a life of your own, you won't be happy even if you date, fall in love, and get married. Why? Because you will have nothing to give to the relationship, and you will drain your dating partner (or spouse) completely dry. Sooner or later you will put extraordinary expectations on your other half to fulfill you, complete you, entertain you, and take care of you. No one person can live up to all these expectations! So before you take someone as your serious partner, please follow this most important rule to dating – get your own life. But because we can't tell you what your life will look like, have a look at what a "un-life" looks like.

People who are living a un-life have one thing in common: they have put their lives on hold. They are so concerned with finding someone to meet their needs that their real life has taken a backseat. Some un-lifers just withdraw and completely give up. They have convinced themselves that life isn't worth living without a partner. Whether they are obsessed with finding "the one" or they have given up, they are the ones who have contracted the fatal disease of the un-life. Here are the most common symptoms to look out for, known as the three Deadly D's. Desperate, Dependent, and Depressed.

Desperate people are never attractive, especially when dating. Take the advice of Confucius: "Desperate people sweat, and sweat stinks on anyone." Relax and let nature take its course. Dependant people are unable to make decisions on their own, and they have nothing to give to a relationship. It is also easy for a dependant person to be caught in a relationship that is not healthy, or one that won't end up in happiness. Of course everyone needs to depend on people, but a person infected with the un-life will look to their mate to meet most of their needs and provide a sense of identity. The last symptom to look out for is feelings of depression and loneliness. This can take many forms, but watch for unhappiness, lack of energy, and unfriendliness. The real danger in depression is that it may lead to a downward spiral that will make it hard for you to enjoy the real pleasures of spending time with someone.

So get out there, get a life, and start dating!

　　星期五下午5：30，你刚刚又度过了一个漫长的工作日。你终于回到了家，找了点吃的，可以坐在沙发上，一手拿着电视遥控器，一手拿着信件。 看看信封，是心上人的来信。打开信，这样的一番话赫然出现在眼前：“我想我们没必要再见面了。” 这是一封纸炸弹，而不是爱的蜜语！你的心有如石沉大海，你意识到这个你投入了如此多时间、精力和感情的人已经消失了，你梦想终生拥有的东西结束了，在最开始的震惊之后， 你开始察看电话留言，希望这只是个错误。你期望着亲爱的她会留下信息，或者哪怕只有只言片语来缓解这个打击。但是，一无所有。你感觉深深地受到了伤害，你被抛弃了，你很孤独。

　　几个月过去了，你的情绪没有丝毫的好转。你问自己到底哪里出问题了？该怪谁呢？为什么好事变坏事了呢？终于，一个全新的道理开始浮现出来，你认识到你们关系失败的症结所在：你没有自己的生活。这个人是你的生命；你所有的自我价值倾注在别人身上。你意识到你的生活依赖于别人——你的事业，你的兴趣，你的朋友，全依赖于另外一个人。这样你就不能给你们的关系付出太多，因此当你们的关系结束时，你也就一无所有了。

　　有时候，只有和所爱的人分手时，你才学到了约会中的最有价值的一点——一个人要维持这种关系最重要的东西就是拥有自我，拥有属于自己的生活！当你为了约会或某种关系投入你所有的精力和自尊的时候，你就不再拥有自己的生活了。

　　有自我生活的人不会等待被别人打倒在地；有自我生活的人不会把结婚当作人生的终极目标；有自我生活的人不会总是陶醉于爱和约会中；有自我生活的人不会徘徊在不同的酒吧间只是为了寻找那个“他”。爱和婚姻是重要的人生目标，但是我们必须正确地对待。当浪漫的爱情蒙蔽了你的双眼，或者成了你生命中最重要的东西时，你的麻烦就来了。

这里有一个让你冷静的消息：如果你没有自己的生活，即使你约会、恋爱、结婚，你也不会幸福。为什么呢？因为你不会对爱有任何贡献，你会耗尽你的约会对象（或伴侣）的活力。迟早，你会特别期望你的另一半来满足你、完善你、款待你，照顾你。没有人可以实现所有这些期望！所以，当你认真地想把某个人当成你的伴侣的时候，请遵循这条约会最重要的规则——拥有自我。不过由于我们不能预测你的生活将会是什么样子，那么就来看看"没有生活"会是什么样子吧。

那些没有自我生活的人有一个共同特点：他们自己的生活处于等待中。他们更关注的是找别人来满足他们的需要，以至于他们的真正生活处于次要地位。有些没有自我生活的人甚至退却，乃至彻底放弃。他们确信没有伴侣的生活不算是真正的生活。无论他们是痴迷于找到另一半还是他们放弃了，他们都患上了失去自我的致命弊病。以下就是最常见的症状，人们称之为三个致命点：孤注一掷、依赖别人、消沉气馁。

孤注一掷的人是没有吸引力的，尤其是约会的时候。孔子曾经说过："孤注一掷的人会殃及别人。"放松自己，顺其自然。依赖性强的人不能够自己做决定，他们对相互之间的关系没有奉献。一个依赖性强的人很容易处在一种不健康的关系当中，自然也不会美满。当然，每个人都有依赖别人的需要，但是如果一个人没有了自己的生活，就会期望其伴侣去满足他的需要，以此来证实自己的存在。最后一个症状就是绝望和孤独的感觉。它会以各种形式体现出来，但要特别注意不快乐、没精神和不友好。消沉气馁的真正危险在于它可能会导致情绪的急剧下降，使你很难享受到与别人在一起的真正乐趣。

所以，从这些情绪中走出来，找回自己的生活，开始约会吧！

couch *n.*

长沙发

ease *v.*

减轻，放松

reject *v.*

拒绝

fizzle *v.*

发嘶嘶声，失败

self-esteem *n.*

自尊，自重

sobering *adj.*

使清醒的，使冷静的

live up to

做到

Confucius

孔子

spiral *v.*

盘旋上升（下降）

Your heart sinks into your stomach as you realize that the person who you invested so much time, energy and emotion into has disappeared and ended something that you hoped would last a lifetime.

你的心有如石沉大海，你意识到这个你投入了如此多时间、精力和感情的人已经消失了，你梦想终生拥有的东西结束了。

People with lives are not waiting to be swept off their feet.

有自我生活的人不会等待被别人打倒在地。

When romantic relationships are an obsession or become the most important thing in your life, you've got a problem!

当浪漫的爱情蒙蔽了你的双眼，或者成了你生命中最重要的东西时，你的麻烦就来了。

Desperate people sweat, and sweat stinks on anyone.

孤注一掷的人会殃及别人。

女人的眼泪
A Woman's Tears

Anonymous
佚名

"Why are you crying？"he asked his Mom.

"你为什么哭呀？"他问他的妈妈。

"Because I'm a woman."she told him.

"因为我是个女人。"她告诉他。

"I don't understand."he said.

"我不明白。"他说。

His Mom Just hugged him and said, "And you never will"…

他的妈妈只是搂紧了他说，"你永远也不会"……

Later the little boy asked his father, "Why does mother seem to cry for no reason？"
"All women cry for no reason"was all his Dad could say…

后来这个小孩问他的父亲，"为什么母亲无缘无故地哭？""所有女人都会无缘无故地哭。"他的父亲只能这样说……

The little boy grew up and became a man, still wondering why women cry…

小男孩长成了大男人，依然没有弄明白女人为什么哭……

Finally he put in a call to God.

最后他给上帝拨了个电话。

When God got on the phone，the man said, "God，why do women cry so easily？"
God said…

当上帝接到电话时，这位长大成人的男子问，"上帝，为什么女人那么容易
哭？"上帝说……

"When I made woman she had to be special .I made her shoulders strong enough to
carry the weight of the world；yet gentle enough to give comfort…

"当我创造女人时她必须是特殊的。我让她的肩膀坚强得足以承担这个世界的
重量，但又足够温柔地给人慰藉……

I gave her an inner strength to endure childbirth and the rejection that many times
comes from her children…

我给她内在的力量以承受分娩的剧痛，并忍受孩子们一次又一次的厌弃……

I gave her a hardness that allows her to keep going when everyone else gives up and
take care of her family through fatigue and sickness without complaining…

我给她竖韧使她在人人都放弃时能独自坚持下去，不顾自身的疲惫和病痛毫无
怨言地照料家人……

I gave her the sensitivity to love her children under any and all circumstances，even
when her child has hurt them very badly…

我给她敏感的心，在任何情况下去爱她的儿女，即使他们深深伤害过她……

I gave her strength to carry her husband through his faults and fashioned her from his rib to protect his heart.

我给她力量让她帮助丈夫克服过失，我用他的一根肋骨造出了她来保护他的心。

I gave her wisdom to know that a good husband never hurts his wife，but sometimes tests her strengths and her resolve to stand beside him unfalteringly.

我给她智慧让她明白，好丈夫永不伤害妻子，但有时会考验她的力量和她坚决站在他身旁的决心。

I gave her a tear to shed，it's hers exclusively to use whenever it is needed. It's her only weakness…

我给她眼泪,这眼泪只属于她,需要时便会流下，这是她唯一的弱点……

It's a tear for mankind……"

这是为人类而流下的泪水……"

女人的 32 个秘密

Thirty-two Secrets in Woman

1. Women need to cry. And they won't do it alone unless they know you can hear them.

女人需要哭泣，并且只有在你能听到时才哭。

2. Women especially love a bargain.

女人特别喜欢便宜货。

3. Women love to shop. It is the only area of the world where they're actually in control.

女人喜欢购物,她们觉得那是她们在这个世界上能控制的惟一领域。

4. Women will always ask questions that have no correct answers, in an effort to trap you into feeling guilty.

女人总是问一些没有正确答案的问题,她们想使你有犯罪感。

5. Women love to talk. Silence intimidates them and they feel a need to fill it, even if they have nothing to say.

女人喜欢交谈。沉默使她们不安,她们需要用交谈打破沉默,即使她们没什么可说的。

6. Women need to feel like there are people worse off than they are.

女人需要感觉到别人不如她们。

7.Women hate bugs. Even the strong-willed ones need a man around when there's a spider or a wasp involved.

女人讨厌虫子。当看到一只蜘蛛或黄蜂时,即使意志力很强的女人也需要一个男人在身旁。

8. Women can't keep secrets.

女人不能保守秘密。

9. Women always go to public rest rooms in groups. It gives them a chance to gossip.

女人经常结伴去公共卫生间,这是她们闲谈的好机会。

10. Women can't refuse to answer a ringing phone, no matter what she's doing.

不管女人在做什么，她都不会拒绝接听任何来电。

11. Women never understand why men love toys.

女人永远不会明白男人为什么喜欢玩具。

12. Women think all beer is the same.

女人觉得所有品牌的啤酒都是一个味儿。

13. Women keep three different shampoos in the shower. After a woman showers, the bathroom will smell like a tropical rain forest.

通常,女人的浴室里总放着三种不同的洗发水。她们沐浴后,浴室就散发着热带雨林的味道。

14. Women don't understand the appeal of sports. Men seek entertainment that allows them to escape reality. Women seek entertainment that reminds them of how horrible things could be.

女人不能领略体育节目的魅力。男人从那些能让他们逃离现实的东西中寻找娱乐,女人则从那些能提醒她们现实有多糟糕的东西中寻找娱乐。

15. If a man goes on a seven-day trip, he'll pack five days worth of clothes and will wear some things twice; if a woman goes on a seven-day trip,she'll pack 21 out fits because she doesn't know what she'll feel like wearing each day.

如果一个男人要出门7天,他会带够5天穿的衣服,并且会将一些衣物穿两次。如果一个女人要出门7天,她会带够21天穿的衣服,因为她不知道自己每天喜欢穿什么。

16. Women brush their hair before bed.

女人在睡觉前梳头。

17. Women are paid less than men, except for one field——Modeling.

女人的薪水比男人低，只有一个行业例外——模特。

18. Women are never wrong. Apologizing is the man's responsibility.

女人永远不会犯错。道歉是男人的责任。

19. Women do not know anything about cars, even if they drive car themselves.

女人对汽车一无所知，即使她们自己开车。

20. Women have better rest rooms. They get the nice chairs and red carpet.

女人的卫生间很讲究，那里有精致的椅子和红地毯。

21. Women love cats. Men say they love cats, but when women aren't looking, men kick cats.

女人喜欢猫。男人说他们喜欢猫，但当女人看不见的时候，他们就会踢猫。

22. Women love to talk on the phone. A woman can visit her girl friend for two weeks, and upon returning home, she will call the same friend and they will talk for three hours.

女人喜欢煲电话粥。一个女人去看她的女朋友，她们一起生活了两个星期，她刚刚回家便会给这个女朋友打电话，她们会聊上3个小时。

23. A woman will dress up to go shopping, water the plants, empty the garbage, answer the phone, read a book, or get the mail.

女人做什么事之前都会化妆——购物、给植物浇水、倒垃圾、接电话、读书、收邮件。

24. Women do NOT want an honest answer to the question, "How do I look？"

在这个问题上女人不想得到诚实的答案——"我看上去怎么样？"

25. "Oh, nothing," has an entirely different meaning in woman-language than it does in man-language.

"哦，没什么。"这句话在女人的字典里的意思和在男人字典里的完全不同。

26. All women will say that they are over weight, but don't agree with them about it.

所有女人都会说自己超重，但千万别对此表示赞同。

27. Only women understand the need for "guest towels" and the "good china".

只有女人知道为什么"客用毛巾"和"好瓷器"是必要的。

28. Women want equal centers, but you rarely hear them clamoring to cover the responsibilities that go with those centers.

女人要求享有与男人同样的权利，但你几乎听不到她们吵嚷着要求承担和男人同样的责任。

29. Women can get out of speeding tickets by pouting. This will get men arrested.

面对超速行驶的罚单，噘嘴可以使女人免于处罚，却会使男人被拘留。

30. Women don't really care about a sense of humor in a guy despite claim to the contrary.

女人并不真的在乎男人是否有幽默感，尽管她们声称幽默感很重要。

31.Women will spend hours dressing up to go out, and then they'll go out and spend more time checking out other women. Men can never catch women checking out other men while women will always catch men checking out other women.

女人在出门前将花费数小时化妆，然后她们出门，花更多时间注视其他女人。男人永远不会察觉女人注视着其他男人，而女人总能察觉男人注视着其他女人。

32. The most embarrassing thing for women is to find another woman wearing the same dress at a formal party.

最让女人尴尬的就是在一个正式的聚会上发现另一个女人穿着和自己同样的衣服。

情人节 的来历
The Origin of St. Valentine's Day

There are many opinions as to the origin of Valentine's Day. Some state that it originated from St. Valentine, a Roman who was martyred for refusing to give up Christianity. He died on February 14, 269 A.D., the same day that had been devoted to love lotteries.

Legend also says that St. Valentine left a farewell note for the jailer's daughter, who had become his friend, and signed it "From Your Valentine".

Other aspects of the story say that Saint Valentine served as a priest at the temple

during the reign of Emperor Claudius. Claudius then had Valentine jailed for defying him. In 496 A.D. Pope Gelasius set aside February 14 to honor St. Valentine.

Gradually, February 14 became the date for exchanging love messages and St. Valentine became the patron saint of lovers. The date was marked by sending poems and simple gifts such as flowers. There was often a social gathering or a ball.

In the United States, Miss Esther Howland is given credit for sending the first valentine cards. Commercial valentines were introduced in the 1800's and now the date is very commercialized.

martyr *v.*

杀害，折磨

lottery *n.*

抽彩票(给奖法)

legend *n.*

传说

defy *v.*

不服从，公然反抗

commercialize *v.*

商业化

关于情人节的起源有许多种说法。有些人认为情人节是一个名叫圣·瓦伦丁的人士发起的。他是罗马人，因为拒绝放弃基督教而于公元前269年2月14日惨遭杀害，这一天也正好是全城盛行彩票抽奖的日子。

而另外一种说法更具有传奇色彩，相传圣·瓦伦丁曾留下一本日记给了狱卒的女儿，署名为"你的瓦伦丁"，据说这名狱卒的女儿就是圣·瓦伦丁的情人。

还有其他的说法也颇为有趣。比如说有人认为在克劳迪亚斯君王统治时期，圣·瓦伦丁曾经是一名神父，因为公然挑战克劳迪亚斯君王的权威而入狱。所以公元前496年罗马教皇格莱西亚斯特意将2月14日作为一个特别的日子以纪念圣·瓦伦丁。

此后2月14日就成为人们向自己心仪的人传递信息以示爱意的日子。而圣·瓦伦丁也就成为了为恋爱中的男女们牵线搭桥的人。这天人们会特意做诗或者用一些小礼物送给自己心爱的人。而且人们还会组织各种各样的聚会来庆祝这个特殊的节日。

艾瑟·霍兰德小姐是美国第一位因为发送情人节卡片而受到荣誉奖励的人。早在19世纪初情人节就已处露商业化的端倪，而如今情人节已经完全被商业化了。

Gradually, February 14 became the date for exchanging love messages and St. Valentine became the patron saint of lovers.

此后2月14日就成为人们向自己心仪的人传递信息以示爱意的日子。而圣·瓦伦丁也就成为了为恋爱中的男女们牵线搭桥的人。

The date was marked by sending poems and simple gifts such as flowers.

这天人们会特意做诗或者用一些小礼物送给自己心爱的人。

花语
The Language of Flowers

Every Flower tells a story. A red rose given to a true love, a daisy peeking out of a buttonhole, a bundle of violets handed demurely to a crush, each conveys a different sentiment.

Flower, plants, and herbs have been used as symbols since antiquity, but the romantic custom of using flowers to converse began to flourish in the 19th century. Courting couples used blooms to declare their affection even when the strict etiquette of the times prohibited them from speaking openly, a method of communicating that became neatly an art. An ill considered choice of blooms could leave a suitor's amorous intention misunderstood, whereas the right flower needed no explanation.

The flowing is our guide to select the right blooms that speak for you.

下面是一个送花指南，能让您的心意得到恰如其分地表达。

baby's breath—everlasting love	满天星—天长地久的爱
calla lily—magnificent beauty	马蹄莲—高贵之美
carnation—pure love	康乃馨—纯洁的爱
cornflower—delicacy	矢车菊—小鸟依人
crocus—cheerfulness	藏红花—心情舒畅
daisy—innocence	雏菊—天真无邪
forget-me-not—remember me	勿忘我—记住我
fuchsia—confiding love	倒挂金钟—信赖的爱
ivy—friendship	常春藤—友谊
jasmine—i attach myself to you	茉莉—我心属于你
lilac—first emotions of love	紫丁香—情窦初开
lily of the valley—return of happiness	铃兰—幸福重现
mint—virtue	薄荷—美德
peony—bashful	牡丹—羞涩不安
rose—love	玫瑰—爱情
white rose— I am worthy of you	白玫瑰—我值得你拥有
rosemary—remembrance	迷迭香—往事悠悠
sweet william—sensitivity	美国石竹—敏感
tulip—declaration of love	郁金香—爱的宣言
pink tulip—caring	粉色郁金香—关切
violet—faithfulness	紫罗兰—忠贞不移

　　每种花都有一个故事。红玫瑰给人真爱，雏菊从钮扣孔探出来张望，一束紫罗兰庄严地递送到迷恋对象面前。每种花都传递着不同的情感。

早在古代，花朵、植物和香草就被用作象征物，但直到19世纪用花交换情感的浪漫习俗才开始盛行。即使在礼教严格禁止男女之间公开表达情意的时代，谈情说爱的情侣还是用鲜花表达自己的感情。这种交流方式差不多成为了一门艺术。如果花选择得不得当，示爱者的满腔爱意就会遭到误解，然而正确选择花，就一切尽在不言中了。

demurely *adv*.

庄重地，严肃地；
装作害羞地

crush *n*.

热恋的对象

sentiment *n*.

情感，情绪

antiquity *n*.

古代，古老

converse *v*.

交谈

suitor *n*.

求婚者

世界上最遥远的距离

The Longest Distance in the World

Anonymous
佚名

The furthest distance in the world
Is not between life and death
But when I stand in front of you
Yct you don't know that I love you

**世界上最遥远的距离，不是生与死，
而是我就站在你的面前，你却不知道我爱你。**

The furthest distance in the world
Is not when I stand in front of you
Yet you can't see my love
But when undoubtedly knowing the love from both
Yet can not be together

**世界上最遥远的距离，不是我站在你
面前，你却不知道我爱你，
而是明明知道彼此相爱，却不能在一起，**

The furthest distance in the world

Is not being apart while being in love

But when plainly can not resist the yearning

Yet pretending you have never been in my heart

世界上最遥远的距离，不是明明知道

彼此相爱，却不能在一起，

而是明明无法抵挡这股想念，却还得故意

装作丝毫没有把你放在心里。

The furthest distance in the world

Is not but using one's indifferent hear

To dig an uncrossable river

For the one who loves you

世界上最遥远的距离，不是明明无法抵挡

这股想念，却还得故意装作丝毫没有把你放在心里，

而是用自己冷漠的心对爱你的

人掘了一条无法跨越的沟渠。

约会时的谈话
Date Conversation

There aren't any significant cultural differences between China and North America when it comes to date conversation. Just be natural and spontaneous. You can always tell from someone's body language and voice if they are interested in you and what you are saying.

You go out with a lady (or a man) and you're all tongue-tied, for no reason! There are plenty of things to talk about, so go ahead and be natural. Talk about general things, or keep the conversation going by talking about something that usually interests someone of the opposite sex.

There is no cultural difference in how to carry on a conversation when you're on a date. People are the same everywhere. However, culture might be an interesting topic for discussion, especially if you're dating a foreigner.

在约会话题上，中国和北美之间没有什么很大的文化差异，自然随意就好。你可以从对方的身体语言和语气中察觉到他们是否对你或你的话语感兴趣。

当你和一位女士（或先生）约会时，你总是莫名其妙地变得张口结舌。其实，有很多话题可以聊，放轻松点、放自然就行了。随便谈些事情，或者为了不冷场干脆就谈谈一些异性感兴趣的话题吧。

当你约会时，怎么让谈话继续下去并没有什么文化上的差异。哪儿的人都一样。但文化可能就是个很有趣的话题，尤其是你在和外国人约会时。

和他/她的约会进展顺利，相处融洽！想要进一步的发展吗？可是还不知道对方是不是已经有了男朋友/女朋友，那么该怎么发问呢？又该如何表达自己是想认真地和他/她交往呢？

1. Tell me, do you already have a boyfriend?

你能告诉我，你是否已经有男朋友了？

No, not at the moment.

没有，现在没有。

2. Would you like to have a drink after dinner?

晚饭后喝杯酒怎么样？

I'd like to, but…

我很乐意去，可是……

3. How about we catch a movie then?

我们去看场电影如何？

终于能和自己喜欢的人约会了？那可要好好想想聊天时的话题哟，否则到时候冷场就不好了。快来看看下面的句子吧，一定会帮上你的。

1.Tell me about yourself.

告诉我一些关于你的事情。

2.What're your hobbies?

你都有什么爱好？

I like dancing.

我喜欢跳舞。

3.Where are you from?

你从哪儿来？

I'm from L.A.

我从洛杉矶来。

4.Where did you go to school?

你在哪儿上的学？

5.What do you think of this place?

你觉得这个地方怎么样？

It's wonderful.

这儿太好了！

约会结束了，别忘了跟对方说你过得很愉快，当然，如果你真的感觉很愉快的话。

1.Can I give you a ride home?

我可以开车送你回家吗？

Thank you. That's very nice of you.

谢谢，你真是太好了。

2.Thank you for going out with me. I had a very nice time.

我今天晚上很快乐。谢谢你今晚和我在一起。

3.I would like to see you again.

我想再次见到你。

Same here!

我也是！

回到家后，如果你们是别人介绍认识的，可以对介绍人说出自己的想法啊。

1.We were smitten with each other.

我们一见倾心。

2. We were crazy about each other.

我们都为彼此着迷。

3. We didn't click so well.

我们彼此没有心动的感觉。

4. We didn't get along very well.

我们相处并不十分愉快。

5. There is no chemistry between us.

我们之间没有过电的感觉。

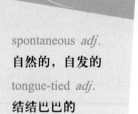

spontaneous *adj.*
自然的，自发的
tongue-tied *adj.*
结结巴巴的

无尽的 爱
A Love without Measure

A heart-warming story tells of a woman who finally decided to ask her boss for a raise in salary. All day she felt nervous and apprehensive. Late in the afternoon she summoned the courage to approach her employer. To her delight, the boss agreed to a raise.

The woman arrived home that evening to a beautiful table set with their best dishes. Candles were softly glowing. Her husband had come home early and prepared a festive meal. She wondered if someone from the office had tipped him off, or ... did he just somehow know that she would not get turned down?

She found him in the kitchen and told him the good news. They embraced and kissed, then sat down to the wonderful meal. Next to her plate the woman found a beautifully lettered note. It read, "Congratulations, darling! I knew you'd get the raise! These things will tell you how much I love you."

Following the supper, her husband went into the kitchen to clean up. She noticed that a second card had fallen from his pocket. Picking it off the floor, she read, "Don't worry about not getting the raise! You deserve it anyway! These things will tell you how much I love you."

Someone has said that the measure of love is when you love without measure. What this man feels for his spouse is total acceptance and love, whether she succeeds or fails. His love celebrates her victories and soothes her wounds. He stands with her, no matter what life throws in their direction.

有一个感人的故事，讲的是有个女人终于决定去向老板提出加薪的要求。她一整天都焦虑不安。下午晚些时候，她鼓起勇气向老板提议。让她感到高兴的是，老板同意给她加薪。

当晚，女人回家后，发现漂亮的餐桌上已经摆满了丰盛的菜肴，烛光在轻轻地摇曳着。丈夫提早回家准备了一顿庆祝宴。她心想，会不会是办公室里有人向他通风报信了呢？或者其他什么原因。他怎么竟知道她不会被拒绝？

她在厨房找到了他，告诉了他这个好消息。他们拥抱亲吻，然后坐下来共享美餐。在她的盘子旁边，女人看到了一张字迹优美的便条。上面写着："祝贺你，亲爱的！我就知道你会加薪的。我为你做的这一切会告诉你，我有多么爱你。"

晚餐后，丈夫到厨房洗碗。她注意到又有张卡片从他口袋里掉了出来。她把卡片从地板上拣起来，念道："不要因为没有加薪而烦恼！不管怎样，是该给你加薪了！我为你做的这一切会告诉你，我有多么爱你。"

有人曾经说过，爱的限度就是无限度地去爱。不管妻子成功还是失败，这个男人都给予她完全的包容和爱。他的爱庆祝她的胜利，也抚平她的创伤。不管生活的道路上遇到什么，他们始终同舟共济。

apprehensive *adj.*

担心的，忧虑的

summon the courage

鼓起勇气

tip off

泄露

soothe *v.*

使(某人，其神经，其情绪)

平静，安慰

She wondered if someone from the office had tipped him off, or... did he just somehow know that she would not get turned down?

她心想，会不会是办公室里有人向他通风报信了呢？或者其他什么原因。他怎么竟知道她不会被拒绝？

Someone has said that the measure of love is when you love without measure.

有人曾经说过，爱的限度就是无限度地去爱。

友情篇

Life is a pure flame, and we live by an invisible sun within us.

生命是把纯净的火焰，我们依靠自己内心看不见的太阳而存在。

理解友情

Understand Friendship

One day, while my ninth grade math teacher, Mr. Pedersen, was reviewing some math concepts with me, my friend Mariam ran by the classroom, stuck her head in the doorway, called out: "Hi Yassee, " and then ran away. Mr. Pedersen looked at me coldly and said with a scowl: "How can you call yourself an Honors student? A real Honors student doesn't associate with people like that!" I wanted to ask him how he could call himself a teacher; after all, a real teacher is supposed to want to help everyone. Instead, I sat silent, stunned by his ignorance and cruelty. He wanted me to drop my childhood friends simply because they didn't place the same importance on schoolwork that I do. If he had thought before speaking, he would have realized that people like him, rather than people like my friends, are better able to turn good students into poor ones by discouraging them with ridiculous comments. I would never slight Mariam. One of my closest friends in freshman year, she was also a below average, non-college bound student. Many of the adults in my life, especially my parents and teachers, would look at those closest to me: Mariam, Alisa, Zena, Lianne, and Marvin, and ask how I could call these "low-life losers" my friends. But such questions show a lack of understanding of the nature of friendship.

Friendship is unconditional and uncritical, based only on mutual respect and the ability to enjoy each other's company. These authority figures never saw the way one of us could do something outrageous, and the rest of us would joke about it for days. We could have fun doing absolutely nothing at all—because the company we provided each other with was enough. Rather than discussing operas, Lewinsky, or the weather, we enjoyed just hanging around each other without any one of us trying to outsmart the others. Still, I realize that these adults had a point to be concerned about the direction my friends were heading; I also was concerned for them, but I wasn't about to leave them. Many times I would advise my friends that some activities may be dangerous or to think things through before doing something, but I would never claim to hold the moral high ground and to condescend to them. When Marvin would begin rolling joints, when Alisa would tell me she skipped school because of a hangover, or when Mariam would tell me that her new boyfriend was in a street gang, I expressed my discomfort with their actions. However, I never blackmailed them with the threat of taking my friendship away. Contrary to the commercials on television, you can have friends who use drugs. In fact, probably everyone does without realizing it.

有一天，九年级的数学老师彼得森先生正和我复习有关数学概念时，朋友玛丽安恰好经过教室，探头叫了一声"嗨，亚斯"就跑开了。彼得森先生冷眼瞧我，皱眉说："你怎么配得上'优秀学生'这个称号呢？真正的'优秀学生'是不会和这些人搅在一起的。"我愣住了。我想问，他又怎样能称得上是真正的老师呢，毕竟，真正的老师应该是乐于帮助别人的。但是，我选择了保持沉默，只是静静地坐着，为其浅薄和冷酷而心惊；他希望我和童年的玩伴划清界线，理由仅仅是因为他们没有像我那样重视学业。如果彼得森先生经过深思熟虑后才说这番话，他就会意识到，不是我的朋友，而是他们这种戴有色眼镜、言辞尖酸刻薄的人更容易让好学生变成差生。我绝不会看不起大学一年级的好友之一玛丽安，虽然她是属于成绩中下，与大学无缘的那种人。我身边的很多成年人，尤其是老师和父母，很难理解我怎么可以和玛丽安、阿莉萨、赞娜、马文这些"彻底的失败者"如此亲密。他们的疑惑恰恰说明他们对友谊本质缺乏理解。

友谊是无条件、不带偏见的；彼此相互尊重，并且喜欢和对方在一起，就是友谊。这些权威人士永远不会明白为什么我们会为一些小事快乐好几天。我们在一起的时候即使什么也不做，也会感到开心——因为大家聚在一起就已足够；不去谈论戏剧、莱温斯基或者天气，大家只是享受那份闲来荡去的惬意，谁也不用绞尽脑汁想着怎样一较高下，分清孰优孰劣。然而，我知道那些大人很担心我朋友的将来；我也有同感，但并没有打算要和他们绝交。所以我常常提醒他们有些活动是很危险的，或是做某件事之前要深思，我绝对不会把道德标准束之高阁而去参与他们其中；当马文想尝试一下大麻的滋味，或者阿莉萨告诉我她因为宿醉而逃课，又或者玛丽安说她的新男友是街上的一个小混混时，我只是为他们感到不安，但我从来没想到以绝交威胁他们。和电视广告不同，你们也可能会结交吸毒的朋友。实际上，也许每个人都有这样的经历，但自己并没有意识到。

scowl *v.*
皱眉头
stun *v.*
使……吃惊
cruelty *n.*
残酷
ridiculous *adj.*
荒唐的
mutual *adj.*
相互的
condescend *v.*
屈尊
hangover *n.*
宿醉
outrageous *adj.*
可耻的

He would have realized that people like him, rather than people like my friends, are better able to turn good students into poor ones by discouraging them with ridiculous comments.

他们这种戴有色眼镜、言辞尖酸刻薄的人更容易让好学生变成差生。

Friendship is unconditional and uncritical, based only on mutual respect and the ability to enjoy each other's company.

友谊是无条件、不带偏见的； 彼此相互尊重，并且喜欢和对方在一起，就是友谊。

一个男孩了和树
A Boy and His Tree

A long time ago, there was a huge apple tree. A little boy loved to come and play around it every day. He climbed to the tree top, ate the apples, and took a nap under the shadow … He loved the tree and the tree loved to play with him.

Time went by…The little boy had grown up and he no longer played around the tree.

One day, the boy came back to the tree and looked sad. "Come and play with me," the tree asked the boy.

"I am no longer a kid, I don't play around trees anymore." The boy replied, "I want toys. I need money to buy them." "Sorry, but I don't have money…but you can pick all my apples and sell them. So, you will have money." The boy was so excited. He picked all the apples on the tree and left happily. The boy didn't come back after he picked the apples. The tree was sad.

One day, the boy returned and the tree was so excited. "Come and play with me." The tree said. "I don't have time to play. I have to work for my family. We need a house for shelter. Can you help me?" "Sorry, but I don't have a house. But you can cut off my branches to build your house." So the boy cut all the branches of the tree and left happily.

The tree was glad to see him happy but the boy didn't appear since then. The tree was again lonely and sad. One hot summer day, the boy returned and the tree was delighted. "Come and play with me!" the tree said.

"I am sad and getting old. I want to go sailing to relax myself. Can you give me a boat?" "Use my trunk to build the boat. You can sail and be happy." So the boy cut the tree trunk to make a boat. He went sailing and did not show up for a long time.

Finally, the boy returned after he left for so many years. "Sorry, my boy. But I don't have anything for you anymore. No more apples for you." the tree said. "I don't have teeth to bite." The boy replied. "No more trunk for you to climb on." "I am too old for that now." the boy said. "I really want to give you something … the only thing left is my dying roots." The tree said with tears. "I don't need much now, just a place to rest. I am tired after all these years." The boy replied. "Good! Old tree roots are the best place to lean on and rest. Come here, please sit down with me and have a rest." The boy sat down and the tree was glad and smiled with tears …

很久以前有一棵高大的苹果树。一个小男孩每天都喜欢来到树旁玩耍。他爬到树顶，吃苹果，在树荫里打盹……他爱这棵树，树也爱和他一起玩。

随着时间的流逝，小男孩长大了，他不再到树旁玩耍了。

一天，男孩回到树旁，看起来很悲伤。"来和我玩吧！"树说。

"我不再是小孩了，我不会再到树下玩耍了。"男孩答到，"我想要玩具，我需要钱来买。"

"很遗憾，我没有钱……但是你可以采摘我的所有苹果拿去卖，这样你就有钱了。"男孩很兴奋。他摘掉树上所有的苹果，然后高兴地离开了。自从那以后男孩没有回来，树很伤心。

一天，男孩回来了，树非常兴奋。"来和我玩吧。"树说。"我没有时间玩，我得为我的家庭工作。我们需要一个房子来遮风挡雨，你能帮我吗？""很遗憾，我没有房子。但是，你可以砍下我的树枝来建房。"因此，男孩砍下所有的树枝，高高兴兴地离开了。

看到他高兴，树也很高兴。但是，自从那时起男孩没再出现，树又孤独、伤心起来。突然，在一个夏日，男孩回到树旁，树很高兴。"来和我玩吧！"树说。

"我很伤心，我开始老了。我想去航海放松自己。你能不能给我一条船？""用我的树干去造一条船，你就能航海了，你会高兴的。"于是，男孩砍倒树干去造船。他航海去了，很长一段时间未露面。

许多年后男孩终于回来了。"很遗憾，我的孩子，我再也没有任何东西可以给你了。没有苹果给你……"树说。"我没有牙齿啃。"男孩答到。"没有树干供你爬。""现在我老了，爬不上去了。"
男孩说。"我真的想把一切都给你……
我惟一剩下的东西是快要死去的树
墩。"树含着眼泪说。"现在，我不需
要什么东西，只需要一个地方来休息。
经过了这些年我太累了。"男孩答到。
"太好了！老树墩就是倚着休息的最好
地方。过来，和我一起坐下休息吧。"
男孩坐下了，树很高兴，含泪而笑……

shelter n.
遮蔽处
branch n.
树枝
trunk n.
树干
tear n.
眼泪
lean v.
倚靠

Time went by…The little boy had grown up and he no longer played around the tree.

随着时间的流逝，小男孩长大了，他不再到树旁玩耍了。

No more trunk for you to climb on.
没有树干供你爬。

I recently lost my best friend Arnold in an automobile accident while moving my family to our new home in Arizona. Arnold was an 8-month-old pot belly who taught me so much about love, devotion and companionship. I am devastated by his loss, but thank God daily for blessing me with the joy of having Arnold for his short life.

Anyone contemplating a pot belly as a pet should know that if you are a true pet lover and devote yourself to them, a pot belly will make the most wonderful friend. You will be assured of endless hours of fascination and entertainment as you both grow together in understanding the human/pot belly relationship. Words cannot describe this relationship and it can only be fully understood by experiencing it.

Arnold didn't know he was a pig — he thought he was just another member of our family — modeling his behavior through observing me, my wife, my two daughters and our beagles. He was convinced he was loved by all; and he was, even when he was ornery trying to just get our attention. He learned his name, how to sit and how to use the litter box all in the first week we had him (at 7 weeks old!).

He loved to sleep on your lap as you sat on the couch watching TV. He didn't care if he grew to weigh 45 lbs, he still expected you to hoist him onto your lap at precisely 8:00 pm every evening where he would fall fast asleep within seconds after snuggling his wet nose between your neck and shoulder.

我最好的朋友阿诺德

My Best Friend Arnold

If you didn't respond to his initial "honks" letting you know it was his nap time, he would bump your legs with his nose until you picked him up. With his weight as it was, you couldn't hold him all evening as he preferred, so you had to slide him off onto the couch next to you where he would sleep for hours with all four legs and his nose sticking straight up in the air. He would snore as long as he could feel you next to him but would immediately wake up if you tried to leave the couch. We had hours of fun balancing objects like a salt shaker on his flat nose while he slept soundly.

Arnold helped me in all my chores around our five acres in the country. Just being there at my feet, interested in what I was doing made even the most mundane tasks enjoyable. When he was out roaming and foraging and you would call out his name, he would come running at top speed, honking the whole way until he got close to you where he would dodge you, zigzagging around with a few victory roles turning in circles before settling down and calmly walking up to you with his tail wagging as if to say (winking) "hah, got-cha."

He even helped me build a kit aircraft and a customized trailer to haul it around in. I was planning on taking him flying with me some day. He loved to play with my sockets and rolled them around on the shop floor. Just as I would struggle and get frustrated with some difficult task, Arnold would show up underneath the trailer, with his wet nose in my ear and honking — seeming to say, "take a break and laugh with me for a while, that should make it all better." And it did, every time. God's marvelous creations minister to us in the most special ways if we can just stop for a few moments and observe them. God used Arnold to teach us this very important lesson in life which we will never forget.

在我们搬家到亚利桑那州的途中发生了交通意外，从此我失去了我最好的朋友阿诺德。阿诺德是一只8个月大的宠物猪，是它令我更懂得爱，懂得投入和维系情谊。它的离去令我悲痛欲绝，不过我还是每天都感谢上帝赐予我与阿诺德相处的那段短暂却快乐的时光。

凡是考虑想养宠物猪的人都应该知道，如果你真心疼它，全身心地伺候它，小猪就会成为你最棒的朋友。在这个与小猪一起探索相处的过程中，你一定会非常着迷，发现其中有无穷的乐趣。言语是无法形容这种关系的，只有亲身经历才能充分体会。

阿诺德并不知道自己是一只猪，它以为自己就是我们家的一员，所以它会观察模仿我、我太太、我两个女儿还有我家小猎犬的一举一动。它深信我们所有人都爱它，事实的确是这样，就算有时候它会耍脾气来吸引我们的注意力，它来到我们家的第一个星期（7周大的时候）就已经学会了自己的名字，学会了怎么坐，还有怎么用那个小盒子。

它喜欢在你坐在沙发上看电视的时候睡在你大腿上。它也不管自己已经长到45磅重，就是要你每天晚上八点准时把它抬到你大腿上来，湿乎乎的鼻子在你的脖子和肩膀之间温存一番后，这家伙就酣睡起来了。开始时候如果你对它"鼾鼾"的睡眠提醒不做反应，它就会用鼻子撞你的脚，直到你把它抱起为止。它倒想一整晚睡在你腿上，但它这么重，你根本是受不了的，所以得把它顺势滑到旁边的沙发上，让它鼻子四脚朝天地呼呼大睡。只要它感觉到你就在它身边，它会放心尽情地打它的鼾；但是一旦你想走开，它会马上醒过来。它沉睡的时候，我们会玩个游戏，在它那扁鼻子上摆像盐瓶那样的小玩艺而要保持平衡不倒，这样一玩就是几个小时，大家玩得不亦乐乎。

在我们那方圆五英亩的乡下地方，阿诺德都会帮我做所有的家务事。只要它挨在你脚跟，兴致勃勃地看你在忙，就足以让最索然无味的杂务变得有趣起来。它在外面溜达觅食的时候，只要你喊它的名字，它就会以最快的速度朝你奔来，"鼾鼾"地一路叫着，跑到离你不远的地方它又会跟你玩起迷藏来，左转右转地走着，绕着圈，一副凯旋而归的模样，然后才静下来慢慢走到你跟前，摇摇尾巴，好像眨着眼跟你说"哈，总算找到你啦！"

它还帮我一起组装了一架小型飞机和一辆运载飞机的特制拖车。我打算哪天把它带上跟我一起飞翔蓝天。它很喜欢玩那些插座零件，在工厂里把它们推来推去。每当我为一些高难度的工作伤透脑筋，灰心丧气的时候，阿诺德就会从拖车的下面钻出来，湿乎乎的鼻子伸到我的耳边，"鼾鼾"地似乎在说"休息一会儿，跟我笑一会儿，然后什么事都好办啦！"果真有效，而且每次都行。只要我们能停一停，仔细看看，就会发现上帝绝妙的创造物总以最特别的方式照顾我们。上帝派阿诺德来给我们上了这人生的重要一课，我们永远不会忘记。

companionship *n.*
友谊
devastate *v.*
毁坏
contemplate *v.*
凝思
ornery *adj.*
卑微的
hoist *v.*
举起（重物）
snuggle *v.*
偎依
chore *n.*
家务杂事
mundane *adj.*
平凡的；平淡的
roam *v.*
漫步
forage *n.*
草料
dodge *v.*
躲避
zigzag *adj.*
曲折的
customized *adj.*
用户化的
minister *v.*
帮助（某人）；
侍候（某人）

I am devastated by his loss, but thank God daily for blessing me with the joy of having Arnold for his short life.

它的离去令我悲痛欲绝，不过我还是每天都感谢上帝赐予我与阿诺德相处的那段短暂却快乐的时光。

God's marvelous creations minister to us in the most special ways if we can just stop for a few moments and observe them.

只要我们能停一停，仔细看看，就会发现上帝绝妙的创造物总以最特别的方式照顾我们。

礼物

The Gift

It was well after mid night, wrapped in my warm fleecy robe I stood silently staring out the ninth floor window of the daunting New York hospital. The morning did come and at nine a.m. on that March 17th, I was wheeled into an operating room. Eleven hours and forty-five minutes later I was wheeled into a recovery room and a very few hours after being returned to my own hospital room I found myself actually on my feet, half walking, half propelled by medical equipment and members of my family. The orders were to walk the length and back of the long hospital corridor.

It was then that I first saw him. I saw him through a haze of, drugs, pain and the dreamy unreality that this could be happening to me. He was standing in the doorway of a hospital room. In my twilight, unfocused state I saw him almost as a spirit shape rather than a full blown person. Yet the body language of this shape was somehow sending out sympathy and encouragement to me.

The next day as I made my scheduled walk, he came out and walked with me to my room. He explained that he and his wife had brought their teenage son to this hospital of hope from Iran. They were still hoping but things were not going well. He told me of how I had encouraged him on that first dreadful night's walking tour and how he was rooting for me. For three more weeks we continued our conversations, each giving the other the gift of caring and friendship. He told me of how he enjoyed seeing my family as they rallied around me and I was saddened by the loneliness of that small family so far from home.

Miraculously, there did come a day when the doctor told me I would be discharged the following morning. That night I told my friend. The next morning he came to my room. I had been up and dressed since dawn. My bright yellow dress gave me hope, and I almost looked human. We talked a bit. I told him I would pray for his son. He thanked me but shrugged his shoulders indicating the hopelessness. We knew we would never see each other again, in this world. This man in his sorrow was so happy for me. I felt his love. He took my hand and said, "You are my sister." I answered back and said, "You are my brother". He turned and left the room.

My family came to retrieve me. Doctors and nurses, to say their goodbyes and give orders. All business had been taken care of. After seven and a half weeks I was leaving the hospital room I had walked into with so much trepidation.

As I turned to walk down the corridor to the elevator, my brother stood in the doorway, smiling, nodding and giving his blessing.

It was 14 years ago today on March 17th 1990 that I entered that operating room and much has happened to the world since my brother and I said our last farewell. Yet I think of him often and he is always in my heart as I feel I am in his. I remember his intense, dark brown eyes as we pledged ourselves as brother and sister. At that moment, I knew without a doubt that the spirit of God hovered over us smiling, nodding and blessing us with the knowledge that we are all one.

　　时间早就过了午夜了，在雄伟威严的纽约医院，我裹在暖暖的羊毛睡袍里，静静地站在九楼病房的窗前凝视窗外。那天还是来了，就在那天，3月17日的早上9点，我被推进了手术室。11个小时45分钟后，我又被推进了疗养室，在被送回自己的病房后，仅仅几个小时，我就已经能下地行走了——一半是自己在走，一半是被医疗器械和家人推着走。按医嘱，我要在医院的长廊里走一个来回。

　　就在那时，我第一次看到他。在药物和疼痛的作用下，透过朦胧的双眼，我看到了他，那景象就如同虚幻的梦境，我也不肯定自己究竟看到了什么。他当时正站在一间病房的门口。我当时正处于那种视力模糊的懵懂状态中，而他对我来说，就像个幽灵，而不是一个完整的人影。但我还是能感觉得到这个影像的身体语言中所流露出的对我的同情和鼓励。

　　第二天，我又按时地在走廊里走动，他从房间里走出来，陪我走回我的病房。他告诉我，他和他的妻子满怀希望地把他十几岁的儿子从伊朗带到这家医院。尽管现在他们还是抱有希望，但情况确实不容乐观。他告诉我，我手术后第一个难熬的晚上艰辛的行走使他受到了鼓舞，他也在暗暗为我加油。在接下来的三个多星期里，我们在一起交谈，互相关心，彼此关爱。他很高兴看到我的家人很关心和支持我，而我也为这个小家庭远离家园的孤单而暗自伤感。

　　就像奇迹一般，终于有一天医生告诉我说，第二天我就可以出院了。那晚，我把这个消息告诉了我的朋友。第二天一早，他来到我的房间。那天，我早早地就起床了，并换好了衣服。那鲜黄色的衣服给了我希望，我总算看起来又像个人了。我们俩谈了一会儿。我对他说，我会为他的儿子祈祷的。他在感谢我的同时，耸了耸肩，流露出失望之情。我们都知道在这个世界上，我们再也不会见面了。这个忧伤的人很为我感到高兴，我能感受到他对我的关爱。他握着我的手说："你就是我的妹妹。" 我回答道："你 就是我的哥哥。"说完，他转过身，走出了房间。

我的家人来接我了。医生和护士向我道别，给我一些嘱咐。所有事情都安排得妥妥当当。在我怀着忐忑不安的心情走进医院的7个半星期后，我终于要离开我的病房了。

就在我沿着走廊向电梯走去时，我哥哥站在他的病房门口，冲我微笑点头，传递着他的祝福。

我进手术室的那天，也就是14年前的今天，1990年3月17日。自从我与我哥哥告别后，这个世界发生了很大的变化。但我还是经常会想起他，他一直都在我的心里，而我相信我也一直在他心中。我记得我们互称兄妹时，他那双真诚的深褐色的眼睛。在那一刻，我知道上帝正在天堂微笑地看着我们，向我们点头，为我们祝福。因为他知道，我们不分彼此。

fleecy *adj.*
蓬松的，羊毛似的
propel *v.*
驱使
root *v.*
使……坚定
rally *v.*
使恢复健康
retrieve *v.*
找回
intense *adj.*
强烈的，热情的

I saw him through a haze of, drugs, pain and the dreamy unreality that this could be happening to me.

在药物和疼痛的作用下，透过朦胧的双眼，我看到了他，那景象就如同虚幻的梦境，我也不肯定自己究竟看到了什么。

At that moment, I knew without a doubt that the Spirit of God hovered over us smiling, nodding and blessing us with the knowledge that we are all one.

在那一刻，我知道上帝正在天堂微笑地看着我们，向我们点头，为我们祝福。因为他知道，我们不分彼此。

独 唱 曲
The Aria

My fiancée and I were out to dinner with two of her friends one weekend night. There was a long wait, but we were in no hurry, so we were happy to sit at the bar for a while and have a few drinks. We had some laughs with the bartender, and it came up in conversation that my fiancée sang opera. She has a gorgeous voice, I mean, you would think an angel had come to earth just to sing for you. Anyway, as were joking around, the bartender offered us a round of drinks if she would sing an aria for the whole restaurant (it was, after all, an Italian restaurant and I suppose they thought it might be a real novelty to have an actual opera singer there).

In an instant my fiancée had grabbed my hand, and put me in a chair in the middle of the room. She began to sing and all I could do was to look at her in awe. The restaurant quickly fell silent. Everyone stopped talking, the waitresses have stopped hustling about, the TV in the bar had suddenly been muted, and there was just this gorgeous, pure voice ringing through the entire place. For a moment I was aware of everyone looking at us, but it was only for a moment. I stared at her as she sang to me, and everyone and everything else disappeared. It was one of those moments, and one of those feelings that I simply can't describe, and won't ever forget. She finished the song, and everyone applauded, some yelling "Encore, encore!!" So she sang another song, not just to me this time, but

also to the entire congregation. It was beautiful and gorgeous. Again she was received with great applause.

We went back to our seats, the bartender brought another round, and the restaurant went back to its former state of jingling glasses, clanking plates, and quiet, yet consistent rumble of 100 different conversations all happening at the same time. About five minutes later a lady and her husband came up to the table and introduced themselves. I don't remember their names, but I won't ever forget what happened next. She told my fiancée how beautiful she sounded and made a little light conversation asking about her career plans and what-not. Then, out of the blue she started telling us about her son who had been killed in a car crash not too long ago, and how much she missed him. She said that she had prayed to God every day and every night for a sign from him, and when my fiancée started singing, she thought she sounded just like an angel, and that must be the sign. I asked the lady what her son's name was. When she told me, my heart nearly jumped out of my chest. She said his name was Nicholas. Without thinking, I stood up, offered her my hand and introduced myself. I said "My name is Nicholas, and everything is going to be OK." The lady's eyes welled up with tears while her husband stood behind her with an entirely blank look on his face. It was all I could do to keep from bursting into tears.

It's probably been a year and a half or two years since that night, and I still get tears in my eyes when I think about it. I'm not sure how I feel about that night, but I do know that it changed my life, and that I will never forget it. I've always believed in God, but I had never felt a presence like I did that night, even if only for a very brief moment. Despite that occurrence I still struggle with my faith. I guess I still have some things to work out in myself before I really come to grips with it. My fiancée and I are no longer together. We split up a few months after that night. Despite all the feelings we shared, it simply wasn't enough to keep us together. It takes more than love to make a relationship work. I don't hope for it to work between us anymore. I just accept what is, and what is not. I just try to enjoy the days as they come. I hope that she's doing the same.

　　一个周末的晚上，我和未婚妻以及她的两个朋友一起出去吃饭。餐厅里排着长队，但我们并不急，所以我们高兴地在吧台边坐下，点了一些饮料。我们跟酒吧的服务员聊得很开心。谈话当中，大家讲起了我那会唱歌剧的未婚妻。她那美妙的声线，我是说，当她唱歌时你会觉得是天使下凡为你歌唱。在我们笑闹的时候，酒吧的服务员提议说如果我未婚妻肯为餐厅的客人唱一曲，他将免费提供给我们几个饮料（如果有人在这个意大利餐馆里唱歌剧，那一定会是件新鲜的事情）。

　　我未婚妻马上拉着我，把我带到大厅中间的一张椅子上坐下。她开始唱歌，我吃惊地望着她。餐馆很快静了下来，大家都不说话了。女服务员都放下手中的活，电视也突然间被消声了，只有她那美妙、清亮的歌声萦绕着整个大厅。这时我意识到大家都在看着我们，但只是那么短暂的一刻。她对着我唱的时候，我出神地望着她，好像天地间除了我们俩之外，其他的一切都隐退了。那一刻，以及我当时的心情无法用言语形容，我永远也忘不了那一刻。她唱完之后，喝彩声不断，一些人高呼着："再来一曲，再来一曲！"她又唱了一首——这次不仅是为我而唱，还献给整个餐馆的客人。她的歌声是如此的美妙、动人。再一次，掌声如雷。

　　我们回到自己的座位上，那个酒吧服务员又给我们送上了免费饮料。餐厅又回到之前觥筹交错的情形。虽然100多张餐桌同时有人说话，聚成此起彼伏的嗡嗡声，但这声音并不大声，整个大厅还算安静。5分钟后，一对夫妇走到我们的餐桌前，向我们作自我介绍。我已经忘记他们叫什么名字了，但我决不会忘记接下来发生的事情。那位夫人称赞了我未婚妻的美妙嗓子，然后与我未婚妻轻声交谈了一会儿，问了她有关工作计划等诸如此类的事情。然后，她突然对我们说起不久前车祸丧生的儿子，告诉我们她有多想念他。她说她时刻都祈祷着能收到来自儿子的口信，当我未婚妻开始唱歌时，她觉得她的声音就像天使，这一定是儿子托她捎来的信号。我问了那位夫人她儿子的名字，当她说出儿子的名字时，我的心几乎跳出胸膛。她说他叫尼古拉斯。我不假思索地站起来，伸出手自我介绍说："我叫尼古拉斯，一切都很好"。泪水弥漫了那位夫人的眼睛，她丈夫目瞪口呆地站在她身后。而我也只能强忍泪水。

事情已经过去一年半或两年了，但每当我想起这件事时仍会热泪盈眶。我不大清楚那天晚上我的感觉是怎样的，但我知道它改变了我的生活，我一辈子也忘不了。一直以来我都相信上帝，但那一晚我真正感受到了他的存在，即便只是短暂的一瞬间。事情过去后，我仍然与我的信念作斗争，我觉得在我认真处理一些事情之前我必须付出很大的努力。那晚过后的几个月，我与未婚妻分手了，虽然我们互相爱着对方，但这不足以让我们在一起。仅有爱是不足以维系一段感情的。我不再奢望我们的爱会有结果，我只有接受事实。现在我努力过好每一天，希望她也一样。

bartender *n.*
酒吧男招待
gorgeous *adj.*
非常美丽的；非常好的
hustle *v.*
乱挤
applaud *v.*
赞同，拍手
congregation *n.*
聚集
Jingling and clanking *n.*
叮当声
split up
分开

I've always believed in God, but I had never felt a presence like I did that night, even if only for a very brief moment.

一直以来我都相信上帝，但那一晚我真正感受到了他的存在，即便只是短暂的一瞬间。

Despite all the feelings we shared, it simply wasn't enough to keep us together.

虽然我们互相爱着对方，但这不足以让我们在一起。

沙子和石头
Sand and Stone

The story goes that two friends were walking through the desert. During some point of the journey they had an argument, and one friend slapped the other one in the face.

The one who got slapped felt hurt, but without saying anything, wrote in the sand: "Today my best friend slapped me in the face."

They kept on walking until they found an oasis, where they decided to take a bath. The one who had been slapped got stuck in the mire and started drowning, but the friend saved him.

After he recovered from the near drowning, he wrote on a stone: "Today my best friend saved my life."

The friend who had slapped and saved his best friend asked him, "After I hurt you, you wrote in the sand and now you write on a stone. Why?"

The other friend replied: "When someone hurts us we should write it down in sand where winds of forgiveness can erase it away. But when someone does something good for us, we must engrave it in stone where no wind can ever erase it."

故事是这样的：两个朋友结伴穿越沙漠，旅途中两人争吵了起来，其中一个打了对方一记耳光。

被打的人感到自己受了伤害，但什么也没有说，只是在沙地上写下了这样一句话："今天我最好的朋友打了我耳光"。

argument *n.*
争吵
slap *v.*
扇耳光
oasis *n.*
沙漠中的绿洲
engrave *v.*
雕刻

他们继续前行，看见到处绿洲，他们正打算在那里洗澡时，刚才被打的人不小心陷入了泥潭，开始深陷，他的朋友救了他。

等他从几近淹死的边缘苏醒过来后，他在石头上刻下："今天我最好的朋友救了我的命。"

他的朋友问："为什么我伤你之后，你在沙子上写字，现在却把字刻在石头上？"

他回答道："当有人伤害了我们，我们应该把它写进沙里，宽恕的风会把仇恨抹去。而当有人为我们做了好事，我们应当把它刻在石头上，没有风可以将它抹去。"

The one who had been slapped got stuck in the mire and started drowning, but the friend saved him.

刚才被打的人不小心陷入了泥潭，开始深陷，他的朋友救了他。

When someone hurts us we should write it down in sand where winds of forgiveness can erase it away.

当有人伤害了我们，我们应该把它写进沙里，宽恕的风会把仇恨抹去。

A light drizzle was falling as my sister Jill and I ran out of the Methodist Church, eager to get home and play with the presents that Santa had left for us and our baby sister, Sharon. Across the street from the church was a Pan American gas station where the Greyhound bus stopped. It was closed for Christmas, but I noticed a family standing outside the locked door, huddled under the narrow overhang in an attempt to keep dry. I wondered briefly why they were there but then forgot about them as I raced to keep up with Jill.

Once we got home, there was barely time to enjoy our presents. We had to go off to our grandparents' house for our annual Christmas dinner. As we drove down the highway through town, I noticed that the family was still there, standing outside the closed gas station.

When my father pulled into the service station, I saw that there were five of them: the parents and three children — two girls and a small boy.

My father rolled down his window. "Merry Christmas," he said.

"Howdy," the man replied. He was very tall and had to stoop slightly to peer into the car.

圣诞节的早晨

Christmas Morning

Jill, Sharon, and I stared at the children, and they stared back at us.

"You're waiting on the bus?"my father asked.

The man said that they were. They were going to Birmingham, where he had a brother and prospects of a job.

"Well, that bus isn't going to come along for several hours, and you're getting wet standing here. Winborn's just a couple miles up the road. They've got a shed with a cover there, and some benches,"my father said."Why don't you all get in the car and I'll run you up there."

The man thought about it for a moment, and then he beckoned to his family. They climbed into the car. They had no luggage, only the clothes they were wearing.

Once they settled in, my father looked back over his shoulder and asked the children if Santa had found them yet. Three glum faces mutely gave him his answer.

"Well, I didn't think so," my father said, winking at my mother, "because when I saw Santa this morning, he told me that he was having trouble finding all, and he asked me if he could leave your toys at my house. We'll just go get them before I take you to the bus stop."

All at once, the three children's faces lit up, and they began to bounce around in the back seat, laughing and chattering.

When we got out of the car at our house, the three children ran through the front door and straight to the toys that were spread out under our Christmas tree. One of the girls spied

Jill's doll and immediately hugged it to her. I remember that the little boy grabbed Sharon's ball. And the other girl picked up something of mine. All this happened a long time ago, but the memory of it remains clear. That was the Christmas when my sisters and I learned the joy of making others happy.

My mother noticed that the middle child was wearing a short-sleeved dress, so she gave the girl Jill's only sweater to wear.

My father invited them to join us at our grandparents' for Christmas dinner, but the parents refused. Even when we all tried to talk them into coming, they were firm in their decision.

Back in the car, on the way to Winborn, my father asked the man if he had money for bus fare.

His brother had sent tickets, the man said.

My father reached into his pocket and pulled out two dollars, which was all he had left until his next payday. He pressed the money into the man's hand. The man tried to give it back, but my father insisted. "It'll be late when you get to Birmingham, and these children will be hungry before then. Take it. I've been broke before, and I know what it's like when you can't feed your family."

We left them there at the bus stop in Winborn. As we drove away, I watched out the window as long as I could, looking back at the little girl hugging her new doll.

天上下着毛毛细雨，我和姐姐吉尔跑出卫理公会教堂，满心只想着快点回到家玩圣诞老人给我们和小妹妹莎伦准备的礼物玩具。教堂的对面是泛美油站，灰狗长途汽车在那停站。因为是圣诞节，油站没开，不过我发现在紧锁的站门外站着一家人，他们挤在狭小的檐篷下，想尽量不被雨淋湿。我闪过一个疑问，他们为什么站在那里呢？但在我赶上吉尔的时候也就把这个疑团抛诸脑后了。

回到家后其实根本没时间去尽情玩礼物，因为我们马上又得去爷爷奶奶家共进一年一度的圣诞大餐。在开车经过刚才那条大路时，我看到那一家人仍然站在紧闭的加油站门外。

爸爸把车开到加油站旁停下，我看见那一家总共有5个人：父母和3个孩子——2个女孩跟1个小男孩。

爸爸摇下车窗对他们说："圣诞快乐！"

"你好，"那个男人回了一句。他长得很高，要稍微弯下腰来往我们车里瞧。

我和吉尔、莎伦盯着那几个小孩，他们也瞪眼看着我们。

"你们在等汽车吗？"爸爸问他们。

男人回答说是，他们准备去伯明翰，他有个哥哥在那边，而且期望能谋到一份工作。

"汽车起码要好几个小时后才到这里，站在这儿等车你们都会淋湿的。往前几英里就是温邦站，那儿有个棚屋，有地方避雨，还有些板凳。不如上车我送你们到那里吧。"

男人想了一下然后示意他家人过来。他们钻进车里，除了身上穿着的衣服，他们没有任何行李。

等他们坐好了，爸爸转过头来问那几个孩子，圣诞老人找到他们没有。3张忧郁的脸无声地回答了他。

"我看不是吧，"爸爸边说边向妈妈眨眼暗示，"早上我碰到圣诞老人了，他说找不到你们，想把给你们的礼物暂时放到我们家里来。现在咱们就去拿礼物吧，待会儿我再送你们去车站。"

3个孩子的脸顿时阴霾尽散，还在后排座位蹦蹦跳跳，笑笑嚷嚷起来。

到了我家一下车，那3个孩子穿过大门就直奔摆在圣诞树下的礼物。其中一个小女孩发现了吉尔的洋娃娃，马上把它抱入怀中。我记得那小男孩抓走了莎伦的小球，而另外一个女孩就挑走了一件我的东西。这些都是很久以前的事了，然而回忆起来还是那么清晰，因为在那个圣诞日我和我的姐妹领会到了让别人快乐而获得的愉悦。

妈妈看到他们家老二穿着的裙子是短袖的，便把吉尔仅有的毛衣给了她穿。

爸爸邀请他们一起去爷爷奶奶家吃圣诞大餐，但他们拒绝了。无论怎么说，他们还是坚持拒绝了我们的好意。

回到车里，在去温邦的路上爸爸问那男人有没有钱买车票。

他说哥哥寄了车票来。

爸爸从口袋里掏出仅有的两美元，本来我们要用它熬到下次发工资的，他却把这钱塞到了男人的手里。男人想把钱推回来，但爸爸硬要他收下。"等你们到伯明翰就已经很晚了，路上孩子们会饿的。收下吧，我以前也曾一贫如洗，让家人挨饿的滋味不好受，我知道的。"

把他们送到温邦的车站后，我们就开车离开了。我从车窗回望良久，凝望着那小女孩拥着她的新洋娃娃。

drizzle *n.*
细雨
huddle *v.*
拥挤，蜷缩
attempt *v.*
尝试
stoop *v.*
弯腰
beckon *v.*
招手
glum *adj.*
阴郁的
grab *v.*
攫取
hug *v.*
拥抱

I wondered briefly why they were there but then forgot about them as I raced to keep up with Jill.

我闪过一个疑问，他们为什么站在那里呢？但在我赶上吉尔的时候也就把这个疑团抛诸脑后了。

All this happened a long time ago, but the memory of it remains clear.

这些都是很久以前的事了，然而回忆起来还是那么清晰。

最美丽的心
The Most Beautiful Heart

One day a young man was standing in the middle of the town proclaiming that he had the most beautiful heart in the whole valley. A large crowd gathered, and they all admired his heart for it was perfect. There was not a flaw in it.

Suddenly, an old man appeared and said, "Why, your heart is not nearly as beautiful as mine."

The crowd and the young man looked at the old man's heart. It was full of scars, it had places where pieces had been removed and other pieces put in, but they didn't fit quite right, and there were several jagged edges. In fact, in some places there were deep gouges where whole pieces were missing.

The young man laughed. "Comparing your heart with mine, mine is perfect and yours is a mess of scars."

"Yes," said the old man, "Yours looks perfect but I would never trade with you. You see, every scar represents a person to whom I have given my love. I tear out a piece of my heart and give it to them, and often they give me a piece of their heart that fits into the empty place in my heart. But because the pieces aren't exact, I have some rough edges, which I cherish, because they remind me of the love we shared."

"Sometimes I have given pieces of my heart away, and the other person hasn't returned a piece of his or her heart to me. These are the empty gouges -- giving love is taking a chance. Although these gouges are painful, they stay open, reminding me of the love I have for those people too, and I hope someday they may return and fill the space I have waiting. So now do you see what true beauty is?"

The young man walked up to the old man, reached into his perfect heart, and ripped a piece out. He offered it to the old man.

The old man placed it in his heart, then took a piece from his old scarred heart and placed it in the wound in the young man's heart. It fit, but not perfectly, as there were some jagged edges.

The young man looked at his heart, not perfect anymore but more beautiful than ever, since love from the old man's heart flowed into his.

They embraced and walked away side by side.

一天，一位年轻人站在城镇的中央，宣布他的心是整个山谷中最美丽的心。围观的人很多，他们都称赞年轻人的心的确是完美无缺，并没有一点瑕疵。

突然，一位老人出现在人群中，说："你的心不如我的美丽。"

围观者和年轻人都朝老人的心看去：它布满了伤疤，有的地方被挖去又重新填补上，但修补得不甚完整，留下一些参差不齐的疤痕。实际上，有的地方缺失了整块，甚至露出很深的豁口。

年轻人笑了起来："我们两人的心相比，我的是那么完美，而你的却是一堆伤疤。"

"是的，"老人说，"你的心从表面来看很完美，但我绝不会跟你交换。你看，每个伤疤都代表我为别人献出的一份爱——我掏出一块心给他们，他们常常会掏出自己的一块同赠给我，以填补我的空缺。但由于这些不完全一样，伤口的边缘就留下了疤痕，不过我十分珍惜它们，因为它们使我想起我们共同拥有的爱心。"

"有时我送出了一瓣心，其他人并没有回赠给我，因此就出现了这些豁口——献出爱也是需要冒风险的。尽管这些豁口很疼，我还是让它们敞开着，它们能使我想起我付出的爱。我希望有一天，得到爱的人们能够回来填补上我心里的空间。你现在明白什么是真正的美丽了吧？"

年轻人默默走近老人，把手伸进自己完美的心中，撕下一块来，把它献给这位老人。

老人接过馈赠，把它放进自己的心里。然后他从自己疤痕累累的心里掏出一块，放在年轻人心里的那个伤口上。正好放进去，但不是特别吻合，也出现了一些疤痕。

　　年轻人看着自己的心，看起来不再完美但比以前更美丽了，因为老人心中的爱也流淌到了他的心里。

　　他们拥抱着，肩并肩离开了。

proclaim *v.*
声称，显露
scar *n.*
伤疤
jagged *adj.*
锯齿状的
gouge *n.*
圆凿
rip *v.*
劈开
embrace *v.*
拥抱

Comparing your heart with mine, mine is perfect and yours is a mess of scars.

我们两人的心相比，我的是那么完美，而你的却是一堆伤疤。

Although these gouges are painful, they stay open, reminding me of the love I have for those people too, and I hope someday they may return and fill the space I have waiting.

尽管这些豁口很疼，我还是让它们敞开着，它们能使我想起我付出的爱。我希望有一天，得到爱的人们能够回来填补上我心里的空间。

这些美好不会消逝
These Things Shall Never Die
——Charles Dickens

The pure, the bright, the beautiful,	一切纯洁的，辉煌的，美丽的，
That stirred our hearts in youth,	强烈地震撼着我们年轻的心灵的，
The impulses to wordless prayer,	推动着我们做无言的祷告的，
The dreams of love and truth;	让我们梦想着爱与真理的；
The longing after something's lost,	在失去后为之感到珍惜的，
The spirit's yearning cry,	使灵魂深切地呼喊着的，
The striving after better hopes,	为了更美好的梦想而奋斗着的，
These things can never die.	这些美好不会消逝。

The timid hand stretched forth to aid,　　羞怯地伸出援助的手，

A brother in his need,　　在你的弟兄需要的时候，

A kindly word in grief's dark hour　　伤恸、困难的时候，一句亲切的话，

That proves a friend indeed；　　就足以证明朋友的真心；

The plea for mercy softly breathed,　　轻声地乞求怜悯，

When justice threatens nigh,　　在审判临近的时候，

The sorrow of a contrite heart —　　懊悔的心有一种伤感——

These things shall never die.　　这些美好不会消逝。

Let nothing pass for every hand　　在人间传递温情，

Must find some work to do；　　尽你所能地去做；

Lose not a chance to waken love —　　别错失了唤醒爱的良机——

Be firm, and just ,and true;　　为人要坚定，正直，忠诚；

So shall a light that cannot fade　　如此上方照耀着你的那道光芒

Beam on thee from on high. 就不会消失。

And angel voices say to thee —
These things shall never die.

你将听到天使的声音在说——
这些美好不会消逝。

yearn v.
渴望
timid adj.
胆怯的
plea v.
恳求
contrite adj.
深感悔恨的
fade v.
淡去

The striving after better hopes,

为了更美好的梦想而奋斗着的，

So shall a light that cannot fade

如此上方照耀着你的那道光芒

Beam on thee from on high.

就不会消失。

永远的朋友
A Forever Friend

A friend walk in when the rest of the world walks out.

别人都走开的时候，朋友仍与你在一起。

Sometimes in life,

有时候在生活中，

You find a special friend;

你会找到一个特别的朋友；

Someone who changes your life just by being part of it.

他只是你生活中的一部分内容，却能改变你整个的生活。

Someone who makes you laugh until you can't stop;

他会把你逗得开怀大笑；

Someone who makes you believe that there really is good in the world.

他会让你相信人间有真情。

Someone who convinces you that there really is an unlocked door just waiting for you to open it.

他会让你确信，真的有一扇不加锁的门，在等待着你去开启。

This is Forever Friendship.

这就是永远的友谊。

when you're down,

当你失意，

and the world seems dark and empty,

当世界变得黯淡与空虚，

Your forever friend lifts you up in spirits and makes that dark and empty world, suddenly seem bright and full.

你真正的朋友会让你振作起来，原本黯淡、空虚的世界顿时变得明亮和充实。

Your forever friend gets you through the hard times, the sad times, and the confused times.

你真正的朋友会与你一同度过困难、伤心和烦恼的时刻。

If you turn and walk away,

你转身走开时，

Your forever friend follows,

真正的朋友会紧紧相随，

If you lose your way,
你迷失方向时，

Your forever friend guides you and cheers you on.
真正的朋友会引导你，鼓励你。

Your forever friend holds your hand and tells you that
everything is going to be okay.
真正的朋友会握着你的手，告诉你一切都会好起来的。

And if you find such a friend,
如果你找到了这样的朋友，

You feel happy and complete,
你会快乐，觉得人生完整，

Because you need not worry,
因为你无需再忧虑，

Your have a forever friend for life,
你拥有了一个真正的朋友，

And forever has no end.
永永远远，永无止境。

convince *v.*

使信服

confused *adj.*

迷惑的

guide *v.*

引导

cheer *v.*

使欢乐

Your forever friend lifts you up in spirits and makes that dark and empty world, suddenly seem bright and full.

你真正的朋友会让你振作起来，原本黯淡、空虚的世界顿时变得明亮和充实。

Your forever friend gets you through the hard times, the sad times, and the confused times.

你真正的朋友会与你一同度过困难、伤心和烦恼的时刻。

让 我 们 微 笑

Let Us Smile

The thing that goes the farthest toward making life worthwhile,

That costs the least and does the most, is just a pleasant smile.

The smile that bubbles from the heart that loves its fellow men,

Will drive away the clouds of gloom and coax the sun again.

It's full of worth and goodness, too, with manly kindness blent;

It's worth a million dollars, and it doesn't cost a cent.

There is no room for sadness when we see a cheery smile;

It always has the same good look; it's never out of style;

It nerves us on to try again when failure makes us blue;

The dimples of encouragement are good for me and you.

It pays the highest interest — for it is merely lent;

It's worth a million dollars, and it doesn't cost a cent.

A smile comes very easy — you can wrinkle up with cheer,
A hundred times before you can squeeze out a salty tear;
It ripples out, moreover, to the heartstrings that will tug,
And always leaves an echo that is very like a hug.
So, smile away! Folks understand what by a smile is meant;
It's worth a million dollars, and it doesn't cost a cent.

那最能赋予生命价值、代价最廉而回报最多的东西，
不过一个令人心畅的微笑而已。
由衷地热爱同胞的微笑，
会驱走心头阴郁的乌云，在心底收获一轮艳阳。
它充满价值和美好，混合着坚毅的仁爱之心；
它价值连城却不花一文。
当我们看到喜悦的微笑，忧伤就会一扫而光；
它始终面容姣好，永不落伍；
失败令我们沮丧之时，它鼓励我们再次尝试；
鼓励的笑属于你我大有裨益。
它支付的利息高昂无比——只因它是种借贷形式；
它价值连城却不花一文。
来一个微笑很容易——嘴角欢快翘起来，
你能百次微笑，可难得挤出一滴泪；
它的涟漪深深波及心弦，
总会留下反响，宛若拥抱。
继续微笑吧！谁都懂得它意味着什么；
它价值连城却不花一文。

worthwhile *adj.*
值得做的
bubble *v.*
起泡
gloom *n.*
阴沉
coax *v.*
哄
blend *v.*
混合
squeeze *v.*
挤压
heartstring *n.*
心弦

The smile that bubbles from the heart that loves its fellow men,
Will drive away the clouds of gloom and coax the sun again.
由衷地热爱同胞的微笑，
会驱走心头阴郁的乌云，在心底收获一轮艳阳。

救命的微笑
A Life-saving Smile

I was sure that I was to be killed tomorrow. I became terribly nervous. I fumbled in my pockets to see if there were any cigarettes, which had escaped their search. I found one and because of my shaking hands, I could barely get it to my lips. But I had no matches, they had taken those. "I looked through the bars at my jailer. He did not make eye contact with me. I called out to him "Have you got a light?" He looked at me, shrugged and came over to light my cigarette. As he came close and lit the match, his eyes inadvertently locked with mine. At that moment, I smiled. I don't know why I did that. Perhaps it was nervousness, perhaps it was because, when you get very close, one to another, it is very hard not to smile. In any case, I smiled. In that instant, it was as though a spark jumped across the gap between our two hearts, our two human souls. I know he didn't want to, but my smile leaped through the bars and generated a smile on his lips, too. He lit my cigarette but stayed near, looking at me directly in the eyes and continuing to smile.

I kept smiling at him, now aware of him as a person and not just a jailer. And his looking at me seemed to have a new dimension too. "Do you have kids?" he asked. "Yes, here, here." I took out my wallet and nervously fumbled for the pictures of my family.

He, too, took out the pictures of his family and began to talk about his plans and hopes for them. My eyes filled with tears. I said that I feared that I'd never see my family again, never have the chance to see them grow up. Tears came to his eyes, too. Suddenly, without another word, he unlocked my cell and silently led me out. Out of the jail, quietly and by back routes, out of the town. There, at the edge of town, he released me. And without another word, he turned back toward the town.

My life was saved by a smile. Yes, the smile — the unaffected, unplanned, natural connection between people. I really believe that if that part of you and that part of me could recognize each other, we wouldn't be enemies. We couldn't have hate or envy or fear.

一想到自己明天就没命了，不禁陷入极端的惶恐。我翻遍了口袋看是否有他们没搜走的香烟，终于找到一支，但我的手紧张得不停发抖，连将烟送进嘴里都成问题，我没有火柴，他们也拿走了。我透过铁栏望着外面的警卫，他并没有注意到我在看他，我叫了他一声："能跟你借个火吗？"他转头望着我，耸了耸肩，然后走了过来，点燃我的香烟。当他帮我点火时，他的眼光无意中与我的相接触，这时我突然冲着他微笑。我不知道自己为何有这般反应，也许是过于紧张，或者是当你如此靠近另一个人，你很难不对他微笑。不管是何理由，我对他笑了。就在这一刹那，这抹微笑如同火花般，打破了我们心灵间的隔阂。我知道他不想笑，但受到了我的感染，他的嘴角不自觉地也现出了笑容。他点完火后并没立刻离开，两眼盯着我瞧，脸上仍带着微笑。

我也保持微笑，仿佛他是个朋友，而不是个守着我的警卫。他看着我的眼神好像有了新标准，"你有小孩吗？"他开口问道。"有，你看。"我拿出了皮夹，手忙脚乱地翻出了我的全家福照片。他也掏出了照片，并且开始讲述他对家人的期望与计划。这时我眼中充满了泪水，我说我害怕再也见不到家人，我害怕没机会看着孩子长大。他听了也流下两行眼泪。突然间，他二话不说地打开了牢门，悄悄地带我从后面的小路逃离了监狱，出了小镇，就在小镇的边上，他放了我，之后便转身往回走，不曾留下一句话。

一个微笑居然能救自己一条命。是的，微笑是人与人之间最自然真挚的沟通方式。我真的相信如果我们能用心灵去认识彼此，世间不会有敌人；恨意、妒嫉、恐惧也会不复存在。

fumble v.
摸索
escape v.
逃离
shrug v.
耸肩
dimension n.
（问题或题目的）方面；部分
route n.
路径
envy v.
嫉妒

As he came close and lit the match, his eyes inadvertently locked with mine.
当他帮我点火时，他的眼光无意中与我的相接触。

I said that I feared that I'd never see my family again, never have the chance to see them grow up.
我说我害怕再也见不到家人，我害怕没机会看着孩子长大。

Your friend is your needs answered.

He is your field which you sow with love and reap with thanksgiving.

And he is your board and your fireside.

For you come to him with your hunger, and you seek him for peace.

When your friend speaks his mind you fear not the "nay" in your own mind, nor do you withhold the "ay."

And when he is silent your heart ceases not to listen to his heart;

For without words, in friendship, all thoughts, all desires, all expectations are born and shared.

When you part from your friend, you grieve not;

For that which you love most in him may be clearer in his absence, as the mountain to the climber is clearer from the plain.

And let there be no purpose in friendship save the deepening of the spirit.

For love that seeks aught but the disclosure of its own mystery is not love but a net cast forth, and only the unprofitable is caught.

And let your best be for your friend.

If he must know the ebb of your tide, let him know its flood also.

For what is your friend that you should seek him with hours to kill?

Seek him always with hours to live.

For it is his to fill your need, but not your emptiness.

你的朋友能满足你的需要，你的朋友是你的土地，你在那里怀着爱而播种，含着感谢而收获。

他是你的食粮、柴草：因为你空腹投友，正为寻求温饱，倘若朋友向你畅谈思想，正确与否，请你务必坦率直讲。

假若你的朋友一声不吭，那么你要静听他的心声，因为在友谊里无需言辞，思想和愿望会自生自长。

别离朋友之时，也无需悲伤、忧愁，因为暂别，你对他的情感更胜一筹，犹如登山者看山，比在平原看更清晰、高大。

你们要全心全意增进友谊，不可怀有其他目的。别有寄托的友谊，不是真正的友谊，而是撒入生活海洋里的网，到头来空收无益。

请把最宝贵的东西献给朋友！假若你生活的低潮值得向朋友讲，那么也应该让他知道涨潮情况；在这个世界上，只为消磨时间，那么，他还能算得你的朋友吗？常到充满活力的朋友那里去，只有这样的朋友，才能满足你的需要，只有他才能驱散你心中的空虚与烦躁。

reap *v.*

收获

withhold *v.*

保留

cease *v.*

停止，遏制

unprofitable *adj.*

无利可图的

ebb *v.*

衰退

tide *n.*

潮流

And when he is silent your heart ceases not to listen to his heart.

假若你的朋友一声不吭，那么你要静听他的心声。

一生的友谊 A Lifetime Friendship

Thomas Jefferson and James Madison met in 1776. Could it have been any other year? They worked together to further American Revolution and later to shape the new scheme of government. From the work sprang a friendship perhaps incomparable in intimacy and the trustfulness of collaboration and induration. It lasted 50 years. It included pleasure and utility but over and above them, there were shared purpose, a common end and an enduring goodness on both sides. Four and a half months before he died, when he was ailing, debt-ridden, and worried about his impoverished family, Jefferson wrote to his longtime friend. His words and Madison's reply remind us that friends are friends until death. They also remind us that sometimes a friendship has a bearing on things larger than the friendship itself, for has there ever been a friendship of greater public consequence than this one?

"The friendship which has subsisted between us now half a century, the harmony of our political principles and pursuits have been sources of constant happiness to me through that long period. It's also been a great solace to me to believe that you're engaged in vindicating to posterity the course that we've pursued for preserving to them, in all their purity, their blessings of self-government, which we had assisted in acquiring for them. If ever the earth has beheld a system of administration conducted with a single and steadfast eye to the general interest and happiness of those committed to it, one which, protected by truth, can never known reproach, it is that to which our lives have been devoted. To myself you have been a pillar of support throughout life. Take care of me when dead and be assured that I should leave with you my last affections. "

A week later Madison replied—

"You cannot look back to the long period of our private friendship and political harmony with more affecting recollections than I do. If they are a source of pleasure to you, what aren' t they not to be to me? We cannot be deprived of the happy consciousness of the pure devotion to the public good with Which we discharge the trust committed to us and I indulge a confidence that sufficient evidence will find in its way to another generation to ensure, after we are gone, whatever of justice may be withheld whilst we are here. "

托马斯·杰斐逊和詹姆斯·麦迪逊相识于1776年。为什么偏偏是这一年呢？当时他们开始共同努力推动美国革命，后来又一同为政府拟订新草案。在这些合作中孕育出的友谊是亲密无间、信诚以托、坚不可摧的。这份友谊维持了50年。当中包含有欢乐，有协作，他们更志同道合地朝共同的目标迈进，历经多年从不间断地令彼此受益。在离开人世前四个半月时，杰斐逊重病在身，债台高筑，并为家庭的贫困感到忧心如焚，于是他提笔给这位知心好友写了封信。从他的信以及麦迪逊的回复中，我们可以看到：这两个朋友是一生之交；并且有时候，他们之间的友情意义之大更超越了友情本身，这份友谊给大众带来的深远影响是前所未有的。

"你我之间的友谊迄今已经走过了半个世纪，我们在政治原则与追求上取得的协调在过去的漫漫岁月中为我带来了源源不断的快乐。我感到一大安慰的是，我相信你还在兢兢业业地致力于造福子孙后代的事业——这份事业我们曾为他们争取过，我们也努力要把他们透明自治的优良体制流传下去。希望这世界上有一种治理制度，在执行的时候专门有坚定不移的一只眼睛来审视它，监护大众利益和为之奋斗者的幸福，建立在真理基础上的制度将永远与责难无缘，我们一生所致力的也正在这里。我自己，还有你，毕生都为此鼎力支持。请你照顾我的身后之事，也请相信，我的友情永远和你同在。"

一个星期后，麦迪逊写了回信——

"在过去的漫长岁月中，你我的友谊与一致的政治观，总令我在回想时心中无比感动。它们为你带来欢乐，对我又何尝不是如此？我们肩负人民的信任，为大众福利鞠躬尽瘁，从中获得的幸福感是难以泯灭的。我坚信，无论当前对我们的评判怎样，我们的一切贡献，身后的下一代人必将给予公断。"

intimacy *n.*
亲密
trustfulness *n.*
信任
ailing *adj.*
生病的
debt-ridden *adj.*
负债的
impoverished *adj.*
穷困的
subsist *v.*
生存
solace *n.*
安慰
vindicate *v.*
辩护
posterity *n.*
后裔
deprive *v.*
剥夺
discharge *v.*
清偿
indulge *v.*
纵容

It included pleasure and utility but over and above them, there were shared purpose, a common end and an enduring goodness on both sides.

当中包含有欢乐，有协作，他们更志同道合地朝共同的目标迈进，历经多年从不间断地令彼此受益。

We cannot be deprived of the happy consciousness of the pure devotion to the public good with Which we discharge the trust committed to us and I indulge a confidence that sufficient evidence will find in its way to another generation to ensure, after we are gone, whatever of justice may be withheld whilst we are here.

我们肩负人民的信任，为大众福利鞠躬尽瘁，从中获得的幸福感是难以泯灭的。我坚信，无论当前对我们的评判怎样，我们的一切贡献，身后的下一代人必将给予公断。

I Want to Know

我 想 知 道

Oriah Mountain Dreamer

It doesn't interest me what you do for a living. I want to know what you ache for, and if you dare to dream of meeting your heart's longing.

It doesn't interest me how old you are. I want to know if you will risk looking like a fool for love, for your dreams, for the adventure of being alive.

It doesn't interest me what planets are squaring your moon. I want to know if you have touched the center of your own sorrow, if you have been opened by life's betrayals or have become shriveled and closed from fear of further pain!

I want to know if you can sit with pain, mine or your own, without moving to hide it or fade it or fix it.

I want to know if you can be with joy, mine or your own, if you can dance with wildness and let the ecstasy fill you to the tips of your fingers and toes without cautioning us to be careful, be realistic, or to remember the limitations of being human.

It doesn't interest me if the story you're telling me is true. I want to know if you can disappoint another to be true to yourself; if you can bear the accusation of betrayal and not betray your own soul. I want to know if you can be faithful and therefore be trustworthy.

I want to know if you can see beauty even when it is not pretty every day, and if you can source your life from god's presence. I want to know if you can live with failure, yours and mine, and still stand on the edge of a lake and shout to the silver of the full moon, "Yes!"

It doesn't interest me to know where you live or how much money you have. I want to know if you can get up after a night of grief and despair, weary and bruised to the bone, and do what needs to be done for the children.

It doesn't interest me who you are, how you came to be here. I want to know if you will stand in the center of the fire with me and not shrink back.

It doesn't interest me where or what or with whom you have studied. I want to know what sustains you from the inside when all else falls away. I want to know if you can be alone with yourself, and if you truly like the company you keep in the empty moments.

你以什么为生我不感兴趣。我想知道的是你因什么而痛苦，想知道你是否敢于去梦想满足心灵的渴望。

你的年龄我不感兴趣。我想知道的是你是否甘当傻瓜去追求爱、追求梦想和经历生活的惊险刺激。

是什么磨圆了你的棱角我不感兴趣。我想知道的是你是否触碰过自己受伤的心，是否因为生活辜负过你而变得豁达，还是因为害怕遭受更多的痛苦而变得无助、紧闭心扉。

我想知道你是否能痛苦着我的痛苦而不是避开它，躲着它。

我想知道你是否能欢乐着我的欢乐，是否能狂舞一曲，让快乐溢满你的指尖和脚趾，而不是告诫我们：要小心翼翼、要现实、要牢记做人的局限。

你说的是真是假我不感兴趣。我想知道的是你是否为了忠实于自己而敢于令他人失望，是否敢于承担背叛的骂名而不愿违背良心，是否能做到诚实可靠从而值得信赖。

我想知道你是否能领略美，是否因为生命的存在而追溯生命的起源，我想知道你是否愿意接受你我的失败并仍然敢于站在湖边，对着银色的满月大声回答"是"。

你栖身何处、有多少金钱我不感兴趣。我想知道的是一夜伤心和绝望、一身疲惫和伤痕之后，你是否照样起床，履行应尽的义务，养育待哺的孩子。

你有何背景、何以成为现在的你我不感兴趣。我想知道的是你是否愿意与我一道，站在烈火中央而不退缩。

114 你在哪里受的教育，学的什么以及与谁为师我不感兴趣。我想知道的是一切消逝之后是什么在内心支撑着你，你是否能够独自面对自己，是否真正喜欢你在空虚的时刻结交的伙伴。

ache *n.*

(持续而隐约的)疼痛

adventure *n.*

冒险

betrayal *n.*

背叛

shrivel *v.*

使束手无策

accusation *n.*

谴责

trustworthy *adj.*

可信赖的

bruise *v.*

打伤，撞伤

sustain *v.*

支撑，维持

I want to know if you have touched the center of your own sorrow, if you have been opened by life's betrayals or have become shriveled and closed from fear of further pain!

我想知道的是你是否触碰过自己受伤的心，是否因为生活辜负过你而变得豁达，还是因为害怕遭受更多的痛苦而变得无助、紧闭心扉。

永恒的友谊 friendship lives on

Karen Del Tufo

Twenty-one years ago, my husband gave me Sam, an eight-week-old schnauzer, to help ease the loss of our daughter. Sam and I developed a very special bond over the next fourteen years. It seemed nothing that happened could ever change that.

At one point, my husband and I decided to relocate from our New York apartment to a new home in New Jersey. After we were there awhile, our neighbor, whose cat had recently had kittens, asked us if we would like one. We were a little apprehensive about Sam's jealousy and how he would handle his turf being invaded, but we decided to risk it and agreed to take a kitten.

We picked a little, gray, playful ball of fur. It was like having a roadrunner in the house. She raced around chasing imaginary mice and squirrels and vaulted from table to chair in the blink of an eye, so we named her Lightning.

At first, Sam and Lightning were very cautious with each other and kept their distance. But slowly, as the days went on, Lightning started following Sam—up the stairs, down the stairs, into the kitchen to watch him eat, into the living room to watch him sleep. As time slept, it was always together; when they ate, it was always next to each other. When I played with one, the other joined in. If Sam barked at something, Lightning ran to see what it was. When I took either one out of the house, the other was always waiting by the door when we returned. That was the way it was for years.

Then, without any warning, Sam began suffering from convulsions and was diagnosed as having a weak heart. I had no other choice but to have him put down. The pain of making that decision, however, was nothing compared with what I experienced when I had to leave Sam at the vet and walk into our house alone. This time, there was no Sam for Lightning to greet and no way to explain why she would never see her friend again.

In the days that followed, Lightning seemed heart-broken. She could not tell me in words that she was suffering, but I could see the pain and disappointment in her eyes whenever anyone opened the front door, or the hope whenever she heard a dog bark.

The weeks wore on and the cat's sorrow seemed to be lifting. One day as I walked into our living room, I happened to glance down on the floor next to our sofa where we had a sculptured replica of Sam that we had bought a few years before. Lying next to the statue, one arm wrapped around the statue's neck, was Lightning, contentedly sleeping with her best friend.

21年前为了帮助我减轻失去女儿的悲痛，我丈夫给了我山姆。那是条才8周大的德国髯狗。在以后的14年间，山姆和我形成了一种十分特殊的亲密关系。似乎无论发生什么事情都无法改变这种关系。

有一年我和丈夫决定从纽约的公寓搬到新泽西州的新家。住下一段时间后，邻居的猫下了小猫，问我们想不想要一只。我们有点担心山姆会嫉妒，会因领地被侵占而有何举措。不过我们还是决定冒冒风险，答应养一只。

我们挑了只毛茸球似的爱玩的小灰猫。家里像是添了只跑得飞快的走鹃。她到处追逐想象中的老鼠和松鼠，一眨眼的工夫就从桌子上跳到椅子上。所以我们管她叫"闪电"。

一开始，山姆和闪电互相戒备，保持一定距离。后来闪电逐渐开始跟着山姆，上楼、下楼、进厨房瞧它吃东西、进起居室看它睡觉。随着时光的流逝，它们俩成了形影不离的朋友。总是在一起睡觉、一块儿吃东西。我逗一个玩时，另一个也随之参与。如果山姆冲着什么东西吠叫时，闪电就会跑去看个究竟。我带一个出门，回家时另一个总会在门前等着。多年来始终如此。

然而，有一天，事先毫无任何预兆，山姆开始出现痉挛，经诊断是心力衰竭。我别无选择只有让它毫无痛苦地死去。我做这个决定是痛苦的，然而，这与我把山姆留在兽医诊所独自一人走入家门时的痛苦却是无法相比的。这一回，再没有让闪电迎接的山姆了，我也无法跟她解释为什么她永远见不到她的朋友了。

在以后的日子里，闪电像是心碎了。她无法用言语向我们倾诉她的悲痛，但每当有人打开前门时，我从她的眼神可以看到她的痛苦与失望，每当她听到狗叫时，我从她的眼神也可以看到她的希望。

日子一周周过去，猫的悲痛似乎也逐渐减轻。有一天我走进起居室，无意中朝沙发旁的地板看了一眼，那里摆着几年前买的山姆雕塑复制品。闪电一只前腿缠着它的脖子，心满意足地躺在雕像旁边，和她最好的朋友睡在了一起。

schnauzer *n.*

[动]髯狗(德国种,刚毛浓眉)

apprehensive *adj.*

忧虑的，担心的

jealousy *n.*

嫉妒

convulsion *n.*

震撼，动乱，震动，惊厥，痉挛

diagnose *v.*

诊断

In the days that followed, Lightning seemed heart-broken. She could not tell me in words that she was suffering, but I could see the pain and disappointment in her eyes whenever anyone opened the front door, or the hope whenever she heard a dog bark.

在以后的日子里，闪电像是心碎了。她无法用言语向我们倾诉她的悲痛，但每当有人打开前门时，我从她的眼神可以看到她的痛苦与失望，每当她听到狗叫时，我从她的眼神也可以看到她的希望。

重拾旧谊

In search of Brotherhood

I am not really sure when our boundaries went up. Men tend to build walls quietly, without warning. All I know is that when I looked up, we weren't talking anymore. Somehow we had become like strangers.

This rift — a simple misunderstanding magnified by male ego — didn't happen overnight. Men aren't like some women I know; we don't announce that we are cutting each other off. Instead, we just slowly starve the relationship of anything substantive until it fades away.

Me and my buddy had let our friendship evaporate to a point where we hadn't spoken in almost two years. Then one morning my mother called me at work and shared something she'd heard about him. "You know, his wife is sick with cancer," she said.

I had to close my office door. I don't cry often, but the news broke me down. I thought of his wedding day four years ago and a picture I snapped of him beaming at me as he wrapped his bride in his arms. I remember telling my wife that I'd never seen him so happy, so sure about something.

As it hit me that he now faced the possibility of losing his love, a deep sense of shame came over me. I wondered how he was coping and who was helping him through this crisis. I thought how devastated I'd be if my own wife were suffering. And I wondered whether he and I could ever be tight again.

We had always been like family, sharing an unusual history that dated back to the turn of the century when our great-grandparents were pals growing up in a small town not far from Nashville. Both our families migrated north to Detroit for better-paying jobs, and remained close through the generations.

When I was born 36 years ago, he was among my first playmates. As we grew older, we became what we called true boys — real aces, spending most of our time together running the streets, hanging at bars and clubs, watching games and chasing women. Our friendship came so easily that we took it for granted, and when it began to unravel, neither of us had a clue how to mend it.

很难说清从什么时候我们之间开始渐渐疏远的。男人间的隔阂总是产生于无声无息之间，事先没有任何预兆。直到一天蓦然回首时才发现我们不再促膝倾谈，疏远得有些形同陌路了。

这种隔阂并不会在一夜之间突然形成，它是男人的自我中心心理在作祟。男人不会像我认识的一些女人一样宣称断绝彼此的往来，他们会渐渐地淡化彼此的关系，直到这感情慢慢地烟消云散。

　　我与朋友的关系就处在这样的淡却中，两年来，我们没说过一句话。直到一天早上，在上班的时候母亲打来一个电话，告诉我她刚刚知道的关于他的消息："他的妻子患了癌症。"

　　我关上了房门，眼泪流了下来，我很少哭，但这消息让我很心痛。四年前参加他婚礼的情景还历历在目，当时他把新娘拥在怀中，对着我的镜头灿烂地笑。我还记得后来对我妻子说，我从没见过他那么义无反顾、那么幸福。

　　如今，想到他可能会由此失去爱人，我忽然觉得很惭愧。他该如何面对，又有谁会帮他共渡难关呢？如果自己处在这样的境况，该是多么绝望！我们能不能重拾旧谊呢？我不由问自己。

　　我们曾经就像一家人，两家的渊源可追溯到本世纪之初，我们的曾祖父母是同在田纳西州纳什维尔市不远的小镇上一起长大的伙伴。两家后来又都为了寻求更好的工作向北迁移到了底特律，大家仍然保持密切的联系，几代世交。

　　从我出生到现在我36岁，他一直是我从小玩到大的亲密伙伴。我们共同成长，一起度过躁动的青春时光，成天在街头闲逛，流连在酒吧舞台，为球赛呐喊助威，一起追风逐蝶，还自认为是少年风范，男儿本色。我们的友谊仿佛与生俱来，自然得让我们觉得理所当然，以至当裂缝悄然出现，我们竟都不知该如何缝补。

boundary *n.*

边界

rift *n.*

裂缝

magnify *v.*

放大，夸大

substantive *adj.*

实质的

evaporate *v.*

蒸发，消失

beam *v.*

喜笑颜开；面露喜色

pal *n.*

伙伴，朋友

unravel *v.*

拆开

Men aren't like some women I know; we don't announce that we are cutting each other off. Instead, we just slowly starve the relationship of anything substantive until it fades away.

男人不会像我认识的一些女人一样宣称断绝彼此的往来，他们会渐渐地淡化彼此的关系，直到这感情慢慢地烟消云散。

God could not be everywhere and therefore he made mothers.

—Jewish proverb

上帝不能无处不在，因此他创造了母亲。

——犹太谚语

马戏表演前的一幕
Circus

Once, when I was a teenager, my father and I were standing in line to buy tickets for the circus. Finally, there was only one family between us and the ticket counter. This family made a big impression on me. There were eight children, all probably under the age of 12. You could tell they didn't have a lot of money. Their clothes were not expensive, but they were clean. The children were well-behaved, all of them standing in line, two-by-two behind their parents, holding hands. They were excitedly jabbering about the clowns, elephants, and other acts they would see that night. One could sense they had never been to the circus before. It promised to be a highlight of their young lives. The father and mother were at the head of the pack, standing proud as could be.

The mother was holding her husband's hand, looking up at him as if to say, "You're my knight in shining armor." He was smiling and basking in pride, looking back at her as if to reply, "You got that right." The ticket lady asked the father how many tickets he wanted. He proudly responded, "Please let me buy eight children's tickets and two adult tickets so I can take my family to the circus." The ticket lady quoted the price. The man's wife let go of his hand, her head dropped, and his lip began to quiver. The father leaned a little closer and asked, "How much did you say?" The ticket lady again quoted the price. The man didn't have enough money. How was he supposed to turn and tell his eight kids that he didn't have enough money to take them to the circus?

Seeing what was going on, my dad put his hand in his pocket, pulled out a $20 bill and dropped it on the ground. (We were not wealthy in any sense of the word!) My father reached down, picked up the bill, tapped the man on the shoulder and said, "Excuse me, sir, this fell out of your pocket." The man knew what was going on. He wasn't begging for a handout but certainly appreciated the help in a desperate, heartbreaking, embarrassing situation. He looked straight into my dad's eyes, took my dad's hand in both of his, squeezed tightly onto the $20 bill, and with his lip quivering and a tear running down his cheek, he replied, "Thank you, thank you, sir. This really means a lot to me and my family."

My father and I went back to our car and drove home. We didn't go to the circus that night, but we didn't go without.

在我十多岁的时候，有一次父亲带我去看马戏团表演。当时排队买票的队伍很长。等了好长时间，终于我们前面只剩下一家人了。

这一家子给我的印象极深。他们有8个孩子，年龄估计都在12岁以下。显然这不会是一个富裕之家。他们衣着并不华贵，但也整洁体面。孩子们十分乖巧听话，两两一排，手牵手地排在双亲的身后。他们正兴高采烈、叽叽喳喳地讨论着马戏团里的小丑，大象等。凭感觉，这群孩子还从未看过马戏，所以，那可能会是他们过得最精彩的一天。他们的父母亲排在最前面，昂首挺胸地站着。

那位母亲牵着丈夫的手，抬头看着他的脸，好像在说："你就是那穿着闪亮盔甲、保护我的骑士。"那位父亲微笑着，满脸自豪地看着妻子，像是在回答："你说对了。"售票小姐问他想买多少张票。他得意地回答说："请给我八张儿童票和两张成人票，我要带上全家去看马戏。"随后，售票小姐报了价钱。但那位母亲突然松开了握住丈夫的手，低下了头，而那位父亲的嘴唇开始颤抖起来，他往前靠了靠，问道："你刚才说多少钱？"售票小姐重复了一遍价格。他的钱不够。但是他要如何告诉那8个孩子说，他不够钱让他们去看马戏呢？

这时，我父亲把手伸进了衣袋，掏出一张20美元，扔到了地上。（我们绝不是什么有钱人！）接着，爸爸弯下身又捡起了那张钞票，拍了拍前面那位父亲的肩膀，说："对不起，先生，这是从你口袋里掉出来的。"这位先生马上领会了其中的含义。他并不是在乞求施舍，但绝对会感激在这种绝望、伤心和尴尬的窘境向他伸出援手的人。他凝视着爸爸的眼睛，双手握着爸爸的手，攥紧了手里的那20美元。他的嘴唇又颤抖起来，一滴眼泪从脸颊滑落，他回答道，"谢谢，谢谢你，先生。您帮了我和我的全家一个大忙。"

circus *n.*
马戏表演
jabber *v.*
信口闲谈
clown *n.*
小丑
squeeze *v.*
紧握
quiver *v.*
颤抖

最后，我和父亲开车折回了家。虽然那天晚上没有去成马戏团，但是我们却没有白跑一趟。

It promised to be a highlight of their young lives.
那可能是他们过得最精彩的一天。

You're my knight in shining armor.
你就是那穿着闪亮盔甲、保护我的骑士。

The man's wife let go of his hand, her head dropped, and his lip began to quiver.

那位母亲突然松开了握住丈夫的手，低下了头，而那位父亲的嘴唇开始颤抖起来。

He wasn't begging for a handout but certainly appreciated the help in a desperate, heartbreaking, embarrassing situation.

他并不是在乞求施舍，但绝对会感激在这种绝望、伤心和尴尬的窘境向他伸出援手的人。

如果能重新选择，
我始终会选你

"If I Could Have Picked,
I Would Have Picked You."

In the doorway of my home, I looked closely at the face of my 23-year-old son, Daniel, his backpack by his side. We were saying good-bye. In a few hours he would be flying to France. He would be staying there for at least a year to learn another language and experience life in a different country.

It was a transitional time in Daniel's life, a passage, a step from college into the adult world. I wanted to leave him some words that would have some meaning, some significance beyond the moment.

But nothing came from my lips. No sound broke the stillness of my beachside home. Outside, I could hear the shrill cries of sea gulls as they circled the ever changing surf on Long Island. Inside, I stood frozen and quiet, looking into the searching eyes of my son.

What does it matter in the course of a life-time if a father never tells a son what he really thinks of him? But as I stood before Daniel, I knew that it does matter. My father and I loved each other. Yet, I always regretted never hearing him put his feelings into words and never having the memory of that moment. Now, I could feel my palms sweat and my throat tighten. Why is it so hard to tell a son something from the heart? My mouth turned dry, and I knew I would be able to get out only a few words clearly.

"Daniel," I said, "if I could have picked, I would have picked you."

That's all I could say. I wasn't sure he understood what I meant. Then he came toward me and threw his arms around me. For a moment, the world and all its people vanished, and there was just Daniel and me in our home by the sea.

He was saying something, but my eyes misted over, and I couldn't understand what he was saying. All I was aware of was the stubble on his chin as his face pressed against mine. And then, the moment ended. I went to work, and Daniel left a few hours later with his girlfriend.

That was seven weeks ago, and I think about him when I walk along the beach on weekends. Thousands of miles away, somewhere out past the ocean waves breaking on the deserted shore, he might be scurrying across Boulevard Saint Germain, strolling through a musty hallway of the Louvre, bending an elbow in a Left Bank café.

What I had said to Daniel was clumsy and trite. It was nothing. And yet, it was everything.

在家门口，我凝视着23岁的儿子丹尼尔的脸。他的背包就放在身旁，我们即将道别，几个小时之后，他就要飞往法国，在那里待上至少一年的时间。他要学习另一种语言，并在一个全新的国度体验新的生活。

这是丹尼尔生命中的一个过渡时期，也是他从象牙塔进入成人世界踏出的一步。我希望送给他几句话，几句能让他受用终身的话语。

但我竟一句话也说不出来。我们的房子坐落在海边，此刻屋里静寂无声。屋外，海鸥在波涛澎湃的长岛海域上空盘旋，我能听见它们发出的尖叫。我就这样站在屋里，默默地注视着儿子那双困惑的眼睛。

即使一位父亲一辈子都不曾亲口告诉儿子自己对他的看法，那又如何？然而，当我面对着丹尼尔，我知道到这非常重要。我爱我的父亲，他也爱我，但我从未听过他说心里话，更没有这些感人的回忆，为此，我总心怀遗憾。现在，我手心冒汗，喉咙打结。为什么对儿子说几句心里话如此困难？我的嘴唇变得干涩，我想我顶多能够清晰地吐出几个字而已。

"丹尼尔，"我终于说出了一句，"如果上帝让我选择谁是我的儿子，我始终会选你。"

这是我惟一能想到的话了。我不晓得丹尼尔是否理解了这句话，但他扑过来抱住了我。那一刻，世界消失了，只剩下我和丹尼尔站在海边的小屋里。

丹尼尔也在说着什么，但泪水已经模糊了我的双眼，我一个字也没听进去。只是当他的脸向我贴过来时，我感觉到了他下巴的胡子茬。然后，一切恢复原样，我去上班了，丹尼尔几个小时后带着女友离开了。

7个星期过去了，周末在海边散步时我会想起丹尼尔。横跨拍打着这个荒芜海岸的茫茫大海，几千英里之外的某个地方，丹尼尔也许正飞奔着穿越圣热蒙大道，或者在罗浮宫散发着霉味的走廊上徘徊，又或者此时正托着下巴坐在左岸咖啡馆里憩息。

我对丹尼尔说的那些话既晦涩又老套，空洞无文。然而，它却道出了一切。

surf *v.*

冲浪

vanish *v.*

消失

stubble *n.*

胡子茬

chin *n.*

下巴

clumsy *adj.*

笨拙的

trite *adj.*

平庸的

If I could have picked, I would have picked you.

如果上帝让我选择谁是我的儿子，我始终会选你。

I stood frozen and quiet, looking into the searching eyes of my son.

我就这样站在屋里，默默地注视着儿子那双困惑的眼睛。

I always regretted never hearing him put his feelings into words and never having the memory of that moment.

我从未听过他说心里话，更没有这些感人的回忆。

我的繁忙日子 My Busy Day

"Mommy, look!" cried my daughter, Darla, pointing to a chicken hawk soaring through the air.

"Uh huh," I murmured, driving, lost in thought about the tight schedule of my Day.

Disappointment filled her face. "What's the matter, Sweetheart?" I asked, entirely dense.

"Nothing," my seven-year-old daughter said. The moment was gone. Near home, we slowed to search for the albino deer that comes out from behind the thick mass of trees in the early evening. She was nowhere to be seen.

"Tonight, she has too many things to do," I said.

Dinner, baths and phone calls filled the hours until bedtime.

"Come on, Darla, time for bed!" She raced past me up the stairs. Tired, I kissed her on the cheek, said prayers and tucked her in.

"Mom, I forgot to give you something!" she said. My patience was gone.

"Give it to me in the morning," I said, but she shook her head.

"You won't have time in the morning!" she retorted.

"I'll take time," I answered defensively. Sometimes no matter how hard I tried, time flowed through my fingers like sand in an hourglass, never enough. Not enough for her, for my husband, and definitely not enough for me.

She wasn't ready to give up yet. She wrinkled her freckled little nose in anger and swiped away her chestnut brown hair.

"No, you won't! It will be just like today when I told you to look at the hawk. You didn't even listen to what I said."

I was too weary to argue; she hit too close to the truth. "Good night!" I shut her door with a resounding thud.

Later though, her gray-blue gaze filled my vision as I thought about how little time we really had until she was grown and gone.

My husband asked, "Why so glum?" I told him.

"Maybe she's not asleep yet. Why don't you check," he said with all the authority of a parent in the right. I followed his advice, wishing it was my own idea.

I cracked open her door, and the light from the window spilled over her sleeping form. In her hand I could see the remains of a crumpled paper. Slowly I opened her palm to see what the item of our disagreement had been.

Tears filled my eyes. She had torn into small pieces a big red heart with a poem she had written titled, "Why I Love My Mother!"

I carefully removed the tattered pieces. Once the puzzle was put back into place, I read what she had written:

Why I Love My Mother

Although you're busy and you work so hard, you always take time to play, I love you Mommy because I am the biggest part of your busy day!

The words were an arrow straight to the heart. At seven years old, she had the wisdom of Solomon.

Ten minutes later I carried a tray to her room, with two cups of hot chocolate with marshmallows and two peanut butter and jelly sandwiches. When I softly touched her smooth cheek, I could feel my heart burst with love.

Her thick dark lashes lay like fans against her lids as they fluttered, awakened from a dreamless sleep, and she looked at the tray.

"What is that for?" she asked, confused by this late-night intrusion.

"This is for you, because you are the most important part of my busy day!" She smiled and sleepily drank half her cup of chocolate. Then she drifted back to sleep, not really understanding how strongly I meant what I said.

"妈妈，看！"我的女儿达拉喊到，小手指着翱翔在空中的小鹰。

当时我开着车，正想着我当天忙碌的日程安排，便随口"嗯"了一声。

女儿一脸的失望。"乖乖，怎么啦？"我问道，完全不知道发生了什么事。

"没什么，"我那7岁的女儿说道。那不愉快的一刻很快就过去了。快到家了，我放慢了车速，想找那头白化变种鹿。她通常在入夜时出现在那片茂密的树林里。但这次我们却找不到她的影踪。

"小鹿今晚太忙了，"我说。

晚餐、沐浴、电话占据了我睡觉前的所有时间。

"达拉，睡觉了！"她从我身旁跑过，我这时已觉得很疲惫，吻了吻她的脸，说了几句祷告的话后便把她推进房里去。

"妈，我忘了给你些东西！"她说。我当时已经没有耐性再听她说话了。

"明早再给我吧，"我说，但她却摇摇头。

"你明早没时间的，"她反驳道。

"我会抽时间的，"我辩解道。有时候，不管我怎么努力，时间还是像沙漏里的沙子一样从我的指间里流走，似乎永远不够用。我永远没有足够的时间耗在女儿身上，丈夫身上，在自己身上更是如此。

她没打算放弃。她生气地皱了皱长着雀斑的小鼻子，拨弄了一下她那栗色的头发。

"不！你不会有时间的！就像今天我让你看看天上的小鹰的时候，你根本就没留意我在说什么。"

我太累了，不想跟她争论。她说得很对。"晚安！" 我重重地关上了她的门。

夜深了，我眼前仍然浮现着女儿蓝灰色的眸子，我想到在女儿长大成人离开我们之前我们共处的时间已所剩无几。

"怎么这么惆怅呢？"我丈夫问。我跟他说了事情的来龙去脉。

"也许她还没睡着呢。为什么不去看看呢，"丈夫以一种完全家长式的语气说道。我接受了他的建议，要是自己也会这么想就好了。

我把门推开了一道小缝。透过窗户射进的光线刚好照在她身上。我看到她手上揣着张皱皱的纸。我慢慢地摊开她的手掌，想看看究竟是什么东西导致了我们母女的不和。

我的眼睛湿润了。她把一个大大的红心撕成了碎片，上面是她自己写的一首诗：

《为什么我爱妈妈！》

我小心翼翼地拿走那些碎片，并重新拼凑起来。诗是这样写的：

虽然你很忙，而且也做得很辛苦，但你总是抽时间陪我玩。我爱妈咪，因为我是你繁忙日子里最重要的部分。

女儿的话语像箭一样刺痛了我的心，7岁的她居然具备了所罗门的智慧。

10分钟后，我端着一个托盘走进她的房间，托盘上盛着两杯加了棉花糖的热巧克力，两片花生黄油和果冻三明治。轻抚着她的脸颊，我的心里盈满了爱意。

她眨着眼睛，乌黑浓密的睫毛像扇子一样在她睡意惺忪的脸颊上扇动，她看着我的托盘。

"这是给谁弄的？"她问道，对我这深夜的造访感到迷惑。

"是给你弄的，因为你是我繁忙日子里最重要的部分！"她笑了，睡意朦胧地喝了半杯巧克力。然后便又躺下睡了，她并没听出我那句话里饱含的深情。

dense *adj*.
密集的
albino *n*.
白化现象
retort *v*.
回嘴，反驳
hourglass *n*.
沙漏
resound *v*.
回响

thud *n*.
重击
glum *adj*.
忧郁的
crumple *v*.
使(某物)起皱
tattered *adj*.
毁坏的
marshmallow *n*.
松软糖果，棉花糖

Sometimes no matter how hard I tried, time flowed through my fingers like sand in an hourglass, never enough.

有时候，不管我怎么努力，时间还是像沙漏里的沙子一样从我的指间里流走，似乎永远不够用。

When I softly touched her smooth cheek, I could feel my heart burst with love.

轻抚着她的脸颊，我的心里盈满了爱意。

母亲的信件
Mum's Letters

To this day I remember my mum's letters. It all started in December 1941. Every night she sat at the big table in the kitchen and wrote to my brother Johnny, who had been drafted that summer. We had not heard from him since the Japanese attacked Pearl Harbor.

I didn't understand why my mum kept writing Johnny when he never wrote back.

"Wait and see-we'll get a letter from him one day," she claimed. Mum said that there was a direct link from the brain to the written word that was just as strong as the light God has granted us. She trusted that this light would find Johnny.

I don't know if she said that to calm herself, dad or all of us down. But I do know that it helped us stick together, and one day a letter really did arrive. Johnny was alive on an island in the Pacific.

Whenever mum had finished a letter, she gave it to dad for him to post it. Then she put the water on to boil, and we sat down at the table and talked about the good old days when our Italian-American family had been a family of ten: mum, dad and eight children. Five boys and three girls. It is hard to understand that they had all moved away from home to work, enrolled in the army, or got married. All except me.

Around next spring mum had got two more sons to write to. Every evening she wrote three different letters which she gave to me and dad afterwards so we could add our greetings.

"All people in this world are here with one particular purpose," she said. "Apparently, mine is to write letters." She tried to explain why it absorbed her so.

"A letter unites people like nothing else. It can make them cry, it can make them laugh. There is no caress more lovely and warm than a love letter, because it makes the world seem very small, and both sender and receiver become like kings in their own kingdoms. My dear, a letter is life itself!"

Today all mum's letters are lost. But those who got them still talk about her and cherish the memory of her letters in their hearts.

至今我依然记得母亲的信。事情要从1941年12月说起。母亲每晚都坐在厨房的大饭桌旁边,给我弟弟约翰写信。那年夏天约翰应征入伍。自从日本袭击珍珠港以后,他就一直杳无音信。

约翰从未回信,我不明白母亲为何还要坚持写下去。

可母亲还是坚持说:"等着瞧吧,总有一天他会给我们回信的。"她深信思想和文字是直接相连,这种联系就像上帝赋予人类的光芒一样强大,而这道光芒终会照耀到约翰的身上。

虽然我不肯定她是否只是在安慰自己,或是父亲,或者是我们几个孩子,但我们一家人却因此更加亲密。而最终我们终于等到了约翰的回信,原来他驻扎在太平洋的一个岛屿上，安然无恙。

每次母亲写完信，就会把信交给父亲去邮寄。然后她把水烧开，和我们围坐在桌旁，聊聊过去的好日子。从前我们这个意裔的美国家庭可是人丁旺盛：父母亲和我们8个兄弟姐妹——五男三女，济济一堂。现在他们都因工作、入伍或婚姻纷纷离开了家，只有我留下来，想想真觉匪夷所思。

第二年春天，母亲也要开始给另外两个儿子写信了。每天晚上，她先写好三封内容不同的信交给我和父亲，然后我们再加上自己的问候。

母亲试着解释她为何如此沉迷写信，"每个人来到这个世界都有一个目的。显然，我就是来写信的。"

"信无可替代地把人与人连在一起，让人笑，让人哭。一封情书比任何爱抚更令人觉得亲爱和温暖，因为它让世界变小，写信人和收信人都成为自己世界里的国王。亲爱的，信就是生命本身！"

draft v.
应征入伍
calm v.
使平静下来
caress v.
爱抚，拥抱

今天，母亲所有的信已经遗失。但是那些收到信的人仍在谈论她，并把有关信的记忆珍藏在心。

We had not heard from him since the Japanese attacked Pearl Harbor.
自从日本袭击珍珠港以后，他就一直杳无音信。

There was a direct link from the brain to the written word that was just as strong as the light God has granted us.
（她深信）思想和文字是直接相连，这种联系就像上帝赋予人类的光芒一样强大。

A letter unites people like nothing else.
信无可替代地把人与人连在一起。

She put the water on to boil, and we sat down at the table and talked about the good old days when our Italian-American family had been a family of ten: mum, dad and eight children.
她把水烧开，和我们围坐在桌旁，聊聊过去的好日子。从前我们这个意裔的美国家庭可是人丁旺盛：父母亲和我们8个兄弟姐妹。

一生的祝福
---- Lifelong Blessing

A young man was getting ready to graduate from college. For many months he had admired a beautiful sports car in a dealer's showroom, and knowing his father could well afford it, he told him that was all he wanted.

As Graduation Day approached, the young man awaited signs that his father had purchased the car. Finally, on the morning of his graduation, his father called him into his private study. His father told him how proud he was to have such a fine son, and told him how much he loved him. He handed his son a beautiful wrapped gift box. Curious, but somewhat disappointed, the young man opened the box and found a lovely, leather-bound Bible, with the young man's name embossed in gold. Angrily, he raised his voice to his father and said, "With all your money you give me a Bible?" He then stormed out of the house, leaving the Bible.

Many years passed and the young man was very successful in business. He had a beautiful home and a wonderful family, but realizing his father was very old, he thought perhaps he should go to see him. He had not seen him since that Graduation Day. Before he could make the arrangements, he received a telegram telling him his father had passed away, and willed all of his possessions to his son. He needed to come home immediately and take care of things.

When he arrived at his father's house, sudden sadness and regret filled his heart. He began to search through his father's important papers and saw the still new Bible, just as he had left it years ago. With tears, he opened the Bible and began to turn the pages. As he was reading, a car key dropped from the back of the Bible. It had a tag with the dealer's name, the same dealer who had the sports car he had desired. On the tag was the date of his graduation, and the words … "PAID IN FULL".

How many times do we miss blessings because they are not packaged as we expected? I trust you enjoyed this. Do not spoil what you have by desiring what you have not; but remember that what you now have was once among the things you only hoped for.

Sometimes we don't realize the good fortune we have or we could have because we expect "the packaging" to be different. What may appear as bad fortune may in fact be the door that is just waiting to be opened.

从前,有位年轻人即将大学毕业。数月来,他一直渴望得到某汽车商产品陈列室中的一辆跑车。他知道,他那富有的父亲肯定买得起这辆车,于是,他便跟父亲说他很想得到那辆漂亮的跑车。

在毕业典礼即将来临的日子里,年轻人等待着父亲买下跑车的消息。终于,在毕业典礼那天上午,父亲将他叫到自己的书房,告诉他自己非常爱他,有他这么出色的儿子自己感到非常自豪。接着,父亲递给儿子一个包装精美的礼品盒。年轻人感到好奇,但带着些许失望地打开礼品盒,却发现里面是一本精美的精装本《圣经》,上面以黄金凸印着年轻人的名字。看罢,年轻人怒气冲冲地向父亲大喊道:"你有那么多钱,却只给我一本《圣经》?"说完,便丢下《圣经》,愤怒地冲出房子。

多年以后,年轻人已事业有成。他拥有一所漂亮的房子,一个温馨的家庭。但当得知父亲年事已高，他想，或许应该去看看他。自从毕业那天起他就一直不见父亲。就在起程时，他收到一封电报——父亲已逝世，并已立下遗嘱将其所有财产转给儿子。他要立即回父亲家处理后事。

在父亲的房子里，他突然内心感到一阵悲伤与懊悔。他开始仔细搜寻父亲的重要文件，突然发现了那本《圣经》——还跟多年前一样崭新。他噙着泪水打开《圣经》并一页一页地阅读着。忽然，从书的背面掉出一把钥匙。钥匙上挂着一个标签，上面写着一家汽车经销商的名字——正是他曾渴望的那辆跑车的经销商。标签上还有他的毕业日期及"款已付清"的字样。

我们多少次地与祝福擦肩而过，仅仅因为他们没有按我们想象中的样子包装好？我相信，你本该很喜欢它的。不要在渴望得到没有的东西时损坏你已经拥有的东西，要记住一点：你现在所拥有的恰恰正是你曾经一心渴望得到的。

有时，我们并没有意识到我们已经拥有或本该拥有的好运，仅仅因为它的外表与我们想象中的有所不同。其实，表面上看起来像是坏运气的东西或许正是等待开启的幸运之门。

He then stormed out of the house, leaving the Bible.

随后他丢下《圣经》，愤怒地冲出房子。

Do not spoil what you have by desiring what you have not; but remember that what you now have was once among the things you only hoped for.

不要在渴望得到没有的东西时损坏你已经拥有的东西，要记住一点：你现在所拥有的恰恰正是你曾经一心渴望得到的。

What may appear as bad fortune may in fact be the door that is just waiting to be opened.

表面上看起来像是坏运气的东西或许正是等待开启的幸运之门。

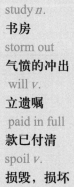

study *n.*
书房
storm out
气愤的冲出
will *v.*
立遗嘱
paid in full
款已付清
spoil *v.*
损毁，损坏

圣诞节的故事 Christmas Story

One afternoon about a week before Christmas, my family of four piled into our minivan to run an errand, and this question came from a small voice in the back seat: "Dad," began my five-year-old son, Patrick, "how come I've never seen you cry?"

Just like that. No preamble. No warning. Surprised, I mumbled something about crying when he wasn't around, but I knew that Patrick had put his young finger on the largest obstacle to my own peace and contentment—the dragon-filled moat separating me from the fullest human expression of joy, sadness and anger. Simply put, I could not cry.

I am scarcely the only man for whom this is true. We men have been conditioned to believe that stoicism is the embodiment of strength. We have traveled through life with stiff upper lips, secretly dying within.

For most of my adult life I have battled depression. Doctors have said much of my problem is physiological, and they have treated it with medication. But I know that my illness is also attributable to years of swallowing rage, sadness, even joy.

148

Strange as it seems, in this world where macho is everything, drunkenness and depression are safer ways for men to deal with feelings than tears. I could only hope the same debilitating handicap would not be passed to the next generation.

So the following day when Patrick and I were in the van after playing at a park, I thanked him for his curiosity. Tears are a good thing, I told him, for boys and girls alike. Crying is God's way of healing people when they're sad. "I'm glad you can cry whenever you're sad," I said. "Sometimes daddies have a harder time showing how they feel. Someday I hope to do better."

Patrick nodded. In truth, I held out little hope. But in the days before Christmas I prayed that somehow I could connect with the dusty core of my own emotions.

"I was wondering if Patrick would sing a verse of 'Away in a Manger' during the service on Christmas Eve," the church youth director asked in a message left on our answering machine.

My wife, Catherine, and I struggled to contain our excitement. Our son's first solo.

Catherine delicately broached the possibility, reminding Patrick how beautifully he sang, telling him how much fun it would be. Patrick himself seemed less convinced and frowned. "You know, Mom," he said, "sometimes when I have to do something important, I get kind of scared."

Grownups feel that way too, he was assured, but the decision was left to him. His deliberations took only a few minutes.

"Okay," Patrick said. "I'll do it."

From the time he was an infant, Patrick has enjoyed an unusual passion for music. By age four he could pound out several bars of "Wagner's Ride of the Valkyries" on the piano.

For the next week Patrick practiced his stanza several times with his mother. A rehearsal at the church went well. Still, I could only envision myself at age five, singing into a microphone before hundreds of people. When Christmas Eve arrived, my expectations were limited.

Catherine, our daughter Melanie and I sat with the congregation in darkness as a spotlight found my son, standing alone at the microphone. He was dressed in white, with a pair of angel wings.

Slowly, confidently, Patrick hit every note. As his voice washed over the people, he seemed a true angel, a true bestower of Christmas miracles.

There was eternity in Patrick's voice that night, a beauty rich enough to penetrate any reserve. At the sound of my son, heavy tears welled at the corners of my eyes.

His song was soon over, and the congregation applauded. Catherine brushed away tears. Melanie sobbed next to me.

After the service, I moved to congratulate Patrick, but he had more urgent priorities. "Mom," he said as his costume was stripped away, "I have to go to the bathroom."

As Patrick disappeared, the pastor wished me a Merry Christmas, but emotion choked off my reply. Outside the sanctuary I received congratulations from fellow church members.

I found my son as he emerged from the bathroom. "Patrick, I need to talk to you about something," I said, smiling. I took him by the hand and led him into a room where we could be alone. I knelt to his height and admired his young face, the large blue eyes, the dusting of freckles on his nose and cheeks, the dimple on one side.

He looked at my moist eyes quizzically.

"Patrick, do you remember when you asked me why you had never seen me cry?"
He nodded.

"Well, I'm crying now."

"Why, Dad?"

"Your singing was so wonderful it made me cry."

Patrick smiled proudly and flew into my arms.

"Sometimes," my son said into my shoulder, "life is so beautiful you have to cry."

Our moment together was over too soon. Untold treasures awaited our five-year-old beneath the tree at home, but I wasn't ready for the traditional plunge into Christmas just yet. I handed Catherine the keys and set off for the mile-long hike home.

The night was cold and crisp. I crossed a park and admired the full moon hanging low over a neighborhood brightly lit in the colors of the season. As I turned toward home, I met a car moving slowly down the street, a family taking in the area's Christmas lights. Someone rolled down a window.

"Merry Christmas," a child's voice yelled out to me.

"Merry Christmas," I yelled back. And the tears began to flow all over again.

在圣诞节前一个星期的某个下午，我们一家四口人挤进自己家的小货车去送货，车后座忽然轻声地传来这样一个问题："爸爸，"我5岁的儿子帕特里克开始问道："我怎么从来没见你哭过呢？"

就是这么唐突，没有前言，没有任何的预示，我感到很错愕。当他不在一旁时，我自言自语地琢磨着哭泣这一话题，但我知道帕特里克那小脑袋已经发现了我心灵深处的一道屏障，那道屏障使我无法获得内心的平静与满足，像一道难以逾越的壕沟，把我从充满人性感情的喜悦、悲哀和生气中隔离开来。直接一点说，我就是不能哭。

其实这种情况并不是只发生在我身上。我们男人已经接受了这种信念，坚忍克己才是力量的体现。在人生道路上，我们总是抿着僵硬的上唇，丝毫不让自己有任何的感情外露，内心的情感不知不觉中已枯竭。

成年后的大部分日子我都在与消沉沮丧抗争。医生都说我的问题主要是生理上的，所以他们给我作药物治疗。但我知道，我的病根在于我多年来对愤怒、悲哀，甚至是欢乐等情感的压抑。

但这似乎也很奇怪，在雄性主宰一切的世界里，在男人处理感情困扰时，酗酒和消沉是比痛哭流涕更安全的方法。我只是希望这种耗损人精神体力的情感障碍不会传给下一代。

所以，第二天，我带帕特里克去公园玩，在驾车返家途中，我对他的好奇表示了谢意。流眼泪是件好事情，我告诉他，无论对于男孩还是女孩，哭泣是当人们悲哀时，上帝拯救他们的方法。"我很高兴，在你觉得伤心的时候，你都能哭出来，"我说，"有时候做爸爸的比较难以表达他们的情感。我希望有一天我会做得更好。"

帕特里克点点头。事实上，我对此不抱什么希望。但圣诞节前的那些日子里，我祈祷着无论如何也要揭开我那尘封的感情了。

"不知道帕特里克是否愿意在平安夜的礼拜仪式上唱〈远处的马槽〉这首圣诗呢，"教堂里主管年轻教徒的神甫在我们的电话留言里问道。

我的妻子凯瑟琳和我都拼命地抑制着内心的兴奋。这是我们的儿子第一次独唱。

凯瑟琳很巧妙地向帕特里克问及这件事的可能性。她提醒帕特里克，他的歌唱得有多动听，告诉他那是多么有趣的事。帕特里克似乎不大相信这些话，他皱着眉头。"你知道的，妈妈，"他说，"有时候，当我要做一件重要的事情时，我总觉得紧张、害怕。"

我们告诉他大人也有这样的感觉，但最后还得由他自己决定。他只沉思了几分钟。

"好吧，"帕特里克说，"我去。"

打从襁褓开始，帕特里克就对音乐表现出不同寻常的热爱。他4岁时，就能在钢琴上敲出瓦格纳的《女武神》的几个小节了。

在接下来的那个星期，帕特里克和他的妈妈把那首圣诗练习了好几次。在教堂里举行的彩排非常成功。相比起来，在我5岁的时候只能想象自己在数百人面前对着麦克风歌唱。而当平安夜到来的时候，我的期望就会落空。

凯瑟琳、我们的女儿梅拉尼、我和其他的信众坐在黑暗当中，当一盏聚光灯掠过时，我找到了我儿子，他一个人站在麦克风前面，白衣飘飘，两侧插着天使的翅膀。

缓缓地、自信地，帕特里克唱准了每一个音符。他的声音陶醉了在座的每一个人，他就像是一个真正的天使，上帝赐予的一件奇迹般的圣诞礼物。

那晚，帕特里克的声音里似乎蕴含着永恒，他的声音圆润得足以穿透世间万物。聆听着儿子的歌声，大颗大颗的泪珠从我眼角涌了出来。

他的歌很快唱完了，大家都鼓起掌来。凯瑟琳擦拭着眼泪，梅拉尼在我身旁哽咽。

礼拜结束后，我去向帕特里克道贺，但他却急着做别的事情。"妈妈，"他一边脱衣服一边说，"我得先去洗手间。"

帕特里克走开后，牧师祝我圣诞快乐，但我激动得一句话也答不上来。在教堂外，我接受了信众们的祝贺。

我找到了我的儿子，当时他正从洗手间出来。"帕特里克，我要和你谈谈。"我微笑着说。我拉着他的手，带他到一个只有我们俩的房间。我蹲下来，和他一般高，欣赏着他那嫩嫩的脸蛋，蓝色的大眼睛，鼻子和两颊有一层雀斑，一边面颊上还有一个小酒窝。

他不解地看着我湿润的双眼。

"帕特里克，你还记得你问过我为什么没有见过我哭吗？"

他点点头。

"嗯，我在哭呢。"

"为什么呢，爸爸？"

"因为你的歌唱得太好了。"

帕特里克自豪地笑着扑进我的怀抱。

"有时候，"我儿子伏在我肩膀上说，"生活会美得让你流泪。"

我们在一起的瞬间太短暂了。家中圣诞树下的那些神秘的礼物正等着我5岁的儿子，但我还没有为一贯以来都匆匆而来的圣诞节做好准备。我把车钥匙递给凯瑟琳，徒步走回一英里以外的家。

那晚的天气干燥寒冷。我穿过公园，在这多彩而快乐的时节，欣赏着挂在半空的满月照耀着万家灯火。当转身回家时，我看见一辆车在街上慢慢地行驶着，原来是一家人在欣赏区内的圣诞灯饰。有人拉下了窗户。

"圣诞快乐。"一个小孩对着我喊。

"圣诞快乐。"我回应道。眼泪又开始流出来了。

minivan *n.*

小型货车

errand *n.*

差使

preamble *n.*

序言

stoicism *n.*

坚忍的态度

embodiment *n.*

化身，体现

physiological *adj.*

生理学的

attributable to

归因于

macho *adj.*

男子气的

debilitate *v.*

使衰弱

broach *v.*

提出话题

deliberation *n.*

熟思，从容

stanza *n.*

一节，比赛中的一环节

congregation *n.*

集合

bestow *v.*

给予

sanctuary *n.*

圣地，圣所

dimple *n.*

酒窝，涟漪

quizzically *adv.*

古怪的

There was eternity in Patrick's voice that night, a beauty rich enough to penetrate any reserve.

那晚，帕特里克的声音里似乎蕴含着永恒，他的声音圆润得足以穿透世间万物。

报 复

Revenge

My grandmother was an iron-willed woman, the feared matriarch of our New York family back in the 1950s.

When I was five years old, she invited some friends and relatives to her Bronx apartment for a party. Among the guests was a neighborhood big shot who was doing well in business. His wife was proud of their social status and let everyone at the party know it. They had a little girl about my age who was spoiled and very much used to getting her own way.

Grandmother spent a lot of time with the big shot and his family. She considered them the most important members of her social circle and worked hard at currying their favor.

At one point during the party, I made my way to the bathroom and closed the door behind me. A minute or two later, the little girl opened the bathroom door and grandly walked in. I was still sitting down.

"Don't you know that little girls aren't supposed to come into the bathroom when a little boy is using it?" I hollered.

The surprise of my being there, along with the indignation I had heaped upon her, stunned the little girl. Then she started to cry. She quickly closed the door, ran to the kitchen, and tearfully complained to her parents and my grandmother.

Most of the partygoers had overheard my loud remark and were greatly amused by it. But not Grandmother.

She was waiting for me when I left the bathroom. I received the longest, sharpest tongue-lashing of my young life. Grandmother yelled that I was impolite and rude and that I had insulted that nice little girl. The guests watched and winced in absolute silence. So forceful was my grandmother's personality that no one dared stand up for me.

After her harangue was over and I had been dismissed, the party continued, but the atmosphere was much more subdued.

Twenty minutes later, all that changed. Grandmother walked by the bathroom and noticed a torrent of water streaming out from under the door.

She shrieked twice — first in astonishment, then in rage. She flung open the bathroom door and saw that the sink and tub were plugged up and that the faucets were going at full blast.

Everyone knew who the culprit was. The guests quickly formed a protective barricade around me, but Grandmother was so furious that she almost got to me anyway, flailing her arms as if trying to swim over the crowd.

Several strong men eventually moved her away and calmed her down, although she sputtered and fumed for quite a while.

My grandfather took me by the hand and sat me on his lap in a chair near the window. He was a kind and gentle man, full of wisdom and patience. Rarely did he raise his voice to anyone, and never did he argue with his wife or defy her wishes.

He looked at me with much curiosity, not at all angry or upset. "Tell me," he asked, "why did you do it?"

"Well, she yelled at me for nothing," I said earnestly. "Now she's got something to yell about."

Grandfather didn't speak right away. He just sat there, looking at me and smiling.
"Eric," he said at last, "you are my revenge."

20世纪50年代我们家住在纽约，当时祖母是一家之主，也是一个令人敬畏的强悍女人。

我5岁那年，她邀请了一些亲戚朋友到布朗克斯的公寓里聚会。在客人中有个做生意发了财的大款，他的妻子神气地向大家炫耀他们家的社会地位。他们有个娇气的小女儿，年纪跟我差不多，脾气很蛮横。

祖母殷勤地伺候着那个大款和他的家人，她把他们看作是她的社交圈里最重要的人物，因此她不遗余力地逢迎他们。

晚会进行中，我走进了洗手间并随手把门关上。大概一两分钟后，我当时还坐在马桶上，那个小女孩推开洗手间的门，大模大样地走了进来。

"难道你不知道当一个男孩在使用洗手间的时候女孩子是不可以进来的吗？"我生气地嚷着说。

听到我生气的吼声，她一下子惊呆了，然后"哇"的一声哭了起来。她飞快地关上门向厨房跑去，边哭边向她的父母和我的祖母告状。

大多数的客人其实都听到了我的怒骂声，他们都被逗乐了，可祖母一点都没笑。

当我从洗手间出来，祖母劈头盖脸地把我骂了一通，骂我没礼貌、少教养、冲撞了那可爱的小女孩。客人们都在静静地看着，我的祖母实在太霸道了，根本没有人敢为我说话。

等她骂完叫我滚开之后，晚会继续进行，但气氛已经大大减弱。

可20分钟之后，一切全都变了。当祖母从洗手间走过的时候，她发现有股水流从门缝里涌出来。

她先是惊异地叫了一声，很快又愤怒地尖叫起来。她猛力地撞开洗手间的门，发现洗手盆和浴缸都被塞子塞住了，水龙头被拧到最大，水正哗啦啦地直流。

每个人都知道是谁搞的鬼，客人们马上在我周围形成了一堵人墙保护我。愤怒的祖母使劲地挥舞着双手，样子就像在人堆里游泳一样。好几次她差点够着我。

最后几个魁梧的男人才把祖母制住，把她拉开让她冷静下来，但她还是气急败坏地嚷了好一阵子。

祖父这时走了过来，牵着我的手到靠窗的一张椅子上坐下，还把我抱到他的膝盖上坐。祖父的性格好，脾气也特别好。他很少提高嗓门和别人说话，也从来没有和祖母吵架，也从来没有违背过祖母的意愿。

他很好奇地打量着我，没有半点生气或烦恼的样子，"告诉我，"他说，"你为什么要这样做呢？"

"是这样的，她先无缘无故地骂了我一顿，"我认真地说，"这回她骂我就有理由了！"

祖父没有马上说话，他只是坐在那儿，笑眯眯地看着我。
最后他终于开口说："艾里克，我的乖孙子，你总算替爷爷出了口气！"

matriarch *n.*

老妇人

holler *v.*

大声叫喊

indignation *n.*

愤慨

heap *v.*

堆积；极力赞扬(批评)某人

lash *v.*

鞭打，讽刺

wince *v.*

退缩

harangue *n.*

没完没了的大声训斥

torrent *n.*

洪流，并发

fling *v.*

投掷

tub *n.*

浴盆

culprit *n.*

犯人

faucet *n.*

龙头

barricade *v.*

设路障，路障

flail *v.*

(使劲地)胡乱挥动；摆动

fume *v.*

发怒；发火

defy *v.*

不服从，蔑视

sputter *v.*

喷溅

revenge *n.*

报仇

Rarely did he raise his voice to anyone, and never did he argue with his wife or defy her wishes.

他很少提高嗓门和别人说话，也从来没有和祖母吵架，也从来没有违背过祖母的意愿。

我记忆中的父亲
Father in Memory

My father was a self-taught mandolin player. He was one of the best string instrument players in our town. He could not read music, but if he heard a tune a few times, he could play it. When he was younger, he was a member of a small country music band. They would play at local dances and on a few occasions would play for the local radio station. He often told us how he had auditioned and earned a position in a band that featured Patsy Cline as their lead singer. He told the family that after he was hired he never went back. Dad was a very religious man. He stated that there was a lot of drinking and cursing the day of his audition and he did not want to be around that type of environment.

Occasionally, Dad would get out his mandolin and play for the family. We three children: Trisha, Monte and I, George Jr., would often sing along. Songs such as the Tennessee Waltz, Harbor Lights and around Christmas time, the well-known rendition of Silver Bells. "Silver Bells, Silver Bells, its Christmas time in the city" would ring throughout the house. One of Dad's favorite hymns was The Old Rugged Cross. We learned the words to the hymn when we were very young, and would sing it with Dad when he would play and sing. Another song that was often shared in our house was a song that accompanied the Walt Disney series: Davey Crockett. Dad only had to hear the song twice before he learned it well enough to play it. "Davey, Davey Crockett, King of the Wild Frontier" was a favorite song for the family. He knew we enjoyed the song and the program and would often get out the mandolin after the program was over. I could never get over how he could play the songs so well after only hearing them a few times. I loved to sing, but I never learned how to play the mandolin. This is something I regret to this day.

Dad loved to play the mandolin for his family he knew we enjoyed singing, and hearing him play. He was like that. If he could give pleasure to others, he would, especially his family. He was always there, sacrificing his time and efforts to see that his family had enough in their life. I had to mature into a man and have children of my own before I realized how much he had sacrificed.

I joined the United States Air Force in January of 1962. Whenever I would come home on leave, I would ask Dad to play the mandolin. Nobody played the mandolin like my father. He could touch your soul with the tones that came out of that old mandolin. He seemed to shine when he was playing. You could see his pride in his ability to play so well for his family.

　　我父亲是个自学成才的曼陀林琴手，他是我们镇最优秀的弦乐演奏者之一。他看不懂乐谱，但是如果听几次曲子，他就能演奏出来。当他年轻一点的时候，他是一个小乡村乐队的成员。他们在当地舞厅演奏，有几次还为当地广播电台演奏。他经常告诉我们，自己如何试演，并在佩茜·克莱恩作为主唱的乐队里赢得一席之位。他告诉家人，一旦被聘用就永不回头。父亲是一个很严谨的人，他讲述了他试演的那天，很多人在喝酒，咒骂，他不想呆在那种环境里。

　　有时候，父亲会拿出曼陀林，为家人弹奏。我们三个小孩：翠莎、蒙蒂和乔治

（也就是我）通常会伴唱，唱的有《田纳西华尔兹》和《海港之光》；到了圣诞节，就唱脍炙人口的《银铃》："银铃，银铃，城里来了圣诞节。"歌声充满了整个房子。父亲最爱的一首赞歌是《古老的十字架》。我们很小的时候就学会歌词了，而且在父亲弹唱的时候，我们也跟着唱。我们经常一起唱的另外一首歌来自沃特·迪斯尼的系列片：《戴维·克罗克特》。父亲只需听两遍就会弹了，"戴维，戴维·克罗克特，荒野边疆的国王。"那是我们家最喜欢的歌曲。他知道我们喜欢那首歌和那个节目，所以每次节目结束后，他就拿出曼陀林弹奏。我永远不能明白他如何能听完几遍后就能把一首曲子弹得那么好。我热爱唱歌，但我没有学会如何弹奏曼陀林，这是我遗憾至今的事情。

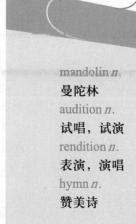

mandolin *n.*
曼陀林
audition *n.*
试唱，试演
rendition *n.*
表演，演唱
hymn *n.*
赞美诗

父亲喜欢为家人弹奏曼陀林，他知道我们喜欢唱歌，喜欢听他弹奏。他就是那样，如果他能把快乐奉献给别人，他从不吝啬，尤其是对他的家人。他总是那样，牺牲自己的时间和精力让家人生活得满足。父亲的这种付出是只有当我长大成人，而且是有了自己的孩子后才能体会到的。

我在1962年1月加入了美国空军。每当我休假回家，我都请求父亲弹奏曼陀林。没有人弹奏曼陀林能达到像我父亲那样的境界，他在那古老的曼陀林上抚出的旋律能够触及你的灵魂。他弹奏的时候，身上似乎能发出四射的光芒。你可以看出，父亲为能给家人弹奏出如此美妙的旋律，他是多么的自豪。

He could touch your soul with the tones that came out of that old mandolin. He seemed to shine when he was playing.

他在那古老的曼陀林上抚出的旋律能够触及你的灵魂。他弹奏的时候，身上似乎能发出四射的光芒。

白色小信封

The Small White Envelope

It's just a small, white envelope stuck among the branches of our Christmas tree. No name, no identification, no inscription. It has peeked through the branches of our tree for the past 10 years or so.

It all began because my husband Mike hated Christmas. He didn't hate the true meaning of Christmas, but the commercial aspects of it; overspending, the frantic running around at the last minute to get a tie for Uncle Harry and the dusting powder for Grandma and the gifts given in desperation because you couldn't think of anything else.

Knowing he felt this way, I decided one year to bypass the usual shirts, sweaters, ties and so forth. I reached for something special just for Mike. The inspiration came in an unusual way.

Our son Kevin, who was 12 that year, was wrestling at the junior level at the school he attended and shortly before Christmas, there was a non-league match against a team sponsored by an inner-city church, mostly black.

These youngsters, dressed in sneakers so ragged that shoestrings seemed to be the only thing holding them together, presented a sharp contrast to our boys in their spiffy blue and gold uniforms and sparkling new wrestling shoes.

As the match began, I was alarmed to see that the other team was wrestling without headgear, a kind of light helmet designed to protect a wrestler's ears.

It was a luxury the ragtag team obviously could not afford. Well, we ended up walloping them. We took every weight class. And as each of their boys got up from the mat, he swaggered around in his tatters with false bravado, a kind of street pride that couldn't acknowledge defeat.

Mike, seated beside me, shook his head sadly, "I wish just one of them could have won," he said. "They have a lot of potential, but losing like this could take the heart right out of them."

Mike loved kids—all kids —and he knew them, having coached little league football, baseball and lacrosse. That's when the idea for his present came.

That afternoon, I went to a local sporting goods store and bought an assortment of wrestling headgear and shoes and sent them anonymously to the inner-city church.

On Christmas Eve, I placed the envelope on the tree, the note inside telling Mike what I had done and that this was his gift from me. His smile was the brightest thing about Christmas that year and in succeeding years.

For each Christmas, I followed the tradition, one year sending a group of mentally handicapped youngsters to a hockey game, another year a check to a pair of elderly brothers whose home had burned to the ground the week before Christmas, and on and on.

我家的圣诞树上挂着一张小小的白色信封。上面既没有收信人的名字和寄信人的签名，也没有任何提示。它挂在我家的圣诞树上已经10多年了。

一切都因丈夫迈克对圣诞的憎恨而起。他并不憎恨圣诞节本身的意义，但他讨厌圣诞被商业化了。人们大把大把地花钱；在平安夜的最后一分钟，围着圈不顾一切地跑去为哈里大叔抢些彩带，为外祖母抢些彩粉；疯狂地瓜分礼物，把一切都抛在脑后。

正是因为知道他的这种感受，于是有一年我决定打破常规（平时都送些衬衣呀、毛衣或是领带等礼物）。我为迈克准备了一些特别的东西。灵感是有来历的。

那年我们的儿子凯文12岁，在学校摔跤队的初级班里接受训练。圣诞节前夕，学校安排了一场非联赛的比赛，对手是本市教会资助的一只队伍，他们大部分队员都是黑人。

这些小伙子们穿着破烂不堪的运动鞋，唯一能够绑在脚上的仿佛只有那条鞋带。而与之形成鲜明对比的是我们的孩子，他们身披金蓝相间的制服，脚蹬崭新的摔跤鞋，显得分外耀眼。

比赛开始了，我惊异地发现对方选手在摔跤的时候没有带专业头盔，只有一种好像质地很薄的帽子保护着选手的耳朵。

对贫民队来说买一顶头盔显然是一种奢侈。毫无疑问我们以绝对的优势获胜，并取得了每个级别的冠军。比赛结束了，他们队的每个男孩从地毯上爬起来，在溃败的失意中昂首阔步装出一副获胜的样子，流露出像街头少年般不愿认输的傲慢。

坐在我身旁的迈克伤心地摇摇头说道："我真希望他们其中一个可以赢。他们很有潜力，就这样输掉了比赛就等于输掉了他们的信心。"

迈克爱孩子——所有的孩子。他曾带过小型的联赛橄榄球队、棒球队和长曲棍球队，所以他了解他们。而我的灵感也由此而发。

当天下午，我就到本地的一家运动用品商店买了摔跤专用的头盔和鞋子，并以匿名的形式把礼物送到了本市的教会。

那个圣诞夜，我把一个信封挂在圣诞树上，里面写着我做的事情，并告诉迈克这是我送给他的礼物。他的笑容是那年圣诞节最明亮的饰物，多少年来那笑容还一直延续着。

每年的圣诞节，我都沿袭了这个传统。我曾送给一群智障儿童一副曲棍球，也曾送给一对年老的兄弟一张支票，因为圣诞节的前一个星期大火烧毁了他们的房子。等等，等等。

identification *n.*

辨认，鉴定，证明，
视为同一

inscription *n.*

题字，碑铭

frantic *adj.*

狂乱的

bypass *v.*

设旁路，迂回

wrestling *v.*

摔跤

non-league

非联赛

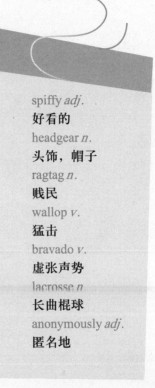

spiffy *adj.*

好看的

headgear *n.*

头饰，帽子

ragtag *n.*

贱民

wallop *v.*

猛击

bravado *v.*

虚张声势

lacrosse *n.*

长曲棍球

anonymously *adj.*

匿名地

As each of their boys got up from the mat, he swaggered around in his tatters with false bravado, a kind of street pride that couldn't acknowledge defeat.

他们队的每个男孩从地毯上爬起来，在溃败的失意中昂首阔步装出一副获胜的样子，流露出像街头少年般不愿认输的傲慢。

不仅仅是位母亲
Not "Just a Mom"

A woman named Emily renewing her driver's license at the County Clerk's office was asked by the woman recorder to state her occupation. She hesitated, uncertain how to classify herself.

"What I mean is," explained the recorder, "do you have a job, or are you just a …"

"Of course I have a job," snapped Emily. "I'm a mother."

"We don't list 'mother' as an occupation … 'Housewife' covers it," said the recorder emphatically.

I forgot all about her story until one day I found myself in the same situation, this time at our own Town Hall. The Clerk was obviously a career woman, poised, efficient, and possessed of a high sounding title like, "Official Interrogator" or "Town Registrar."

"What is your occupation?" she probed.

What made me say it, I do not know ... The words simply popped out. "I'm a Research Associate in the field of Child Development and Human Relations."

The clerk paused, ballpoint pen frozen in midair, and looked up as though she had not heard right.

I repeated the title slowly, emphasizing the most significant words. Then I stared with wonder as my pronouncement was written in bold, black ink on the official questionnaire.

"Might I ask," said the clerk with new interest, "just what you do in your field?"

Coolly, without any trace of fluster in my voice, I heard myself reply, "I have a continuing program of research(what mother doesn't), in the laboratory and in the field (normally I would have said indoors and out). I'm working for my Masters (the whole darned family), and already have four credits (all daughters). Of course, the job is one of the most demanding in the humanities (any mother care to disagree?) and I often work 14 hours a day (24 is more like it). But the job is more challenging than most run-of-the-mill careers and the rewards are more of a satisfaction rather than just money."

There was an increasing note of respect in the clerk's voice as she completed the form, stood up, and personally ushered me to the door.

As I drove into our driveway, buoyed up by my glamorous new career, I was greeted by my lab assistants— ages 13, 7, and 3. Upstairs I could hear our new experimental model (a 6-month-old baby), in the child-development program, testing out a new vocal pattern.

I felt triumphant! I had scored a beat on bureaucracy! And I had gone on the official records as someone more distinguished and indispensable to mankind than "just another mother."

Motherhood … What a glorious career! Especially when there's a title on the door.

一位名叫埃米莉的妇女在县办事处给驾驶执照续期时，一名女记录员问及她的职业。她犹豫了一下，不敢肯定应如何将自己归类。"我意思是说你有没有工作，"那名记录员解释说，"还是说你只不过是一名……"

"我当然有工作，"埃米莉马上回答，"我是一名母亲。"

"我们这里不把'母亲'看成是一个职业……'家庭主妇'就可以了。"那名记录员断然回答。

这个故事听后我就忘了。直到有一天在市政厅，我也遇到了同样的情况。很显然，那名办事员是位职业女性，自信、有能力，并有着一个类似"官方讯问员"或"镇登记员"之类很堂皇的头衔。"你的职业？"她问道。

至今我也不知道，当时是什么因素作怪，我脱口而出："我是儿童发育和人类关系研究员。"

那名办事员愣住了，拿着圆珠笔的手也不动了。她抬头看着我，好像没有听清楚我说什么似的。

我慢慢地把我的职业再重复一遍，在说到重要的词时还加重语气。然后，我惊奇地看着我的话被粗黑的笔记录在官方的问卷上。

"我能不能问一下，"这名办事员好奇地问，"你在这个领域具体做什么？"

我非常镇定地答道："我有一个不间断的研究项目（哪位母亲不是这样呢？），工作地点包括实验室和现场（通常我会说室内和户外）。我在为我的学位努力（就是我们一家人），而且已经有了四个学分（全部是女儿）。当然，我的工作是人类要求最高的工作之一（有哪位母亲会反对吗？）而且我通常工作一天14小时（24小时更为准确）。但这项工作比大部分普通工作都具有挑战性，而它通常带来的回报不是金钱，更多的是满足感。"

那名办事员在填完表格后，站起来，亲自把我送到门口。在这个过程中，她说话时流露出一股敬意。

我回到家，把车停在家门前的车道时，还对自己响亮的头衔觉得飘飘然。我那三名年龄分别为13岁、7岁、3岁的实验室助手正在等着我，从楼上传来我们的新实验模特儿（6个月大的婴儿）的声音，她正放开嗓门，测试着新的声音模式。

我感到欢欣鼓舞！我竟然打败了官僚机构！如今，在官方的纪录上，我成了人类超群出众、不可或缺的人物，而不仅仅是一位母亲。

母亲，多么荣耀的一项职业！尤其是当它还有一个动听的头衔。

renew v.
使更新

emphatically adv.
强调地

poise v.
使平衡

probe v.
调查

pop adj.
流行的

emphasize v.
强调

questionnaire n.
问卷

fluster v.
慌乱，使慌乱

usher v.
引导

buoy v.
使浮起

glamorous adj.
迷人的

bureaucracy n.
办公署

triumphant adj.
胜利的

distinguished adj.
卓著的

indispensable adj.
不可缺少的

glorious adj.
光荣的

The clerk paused, ballpoint pen frozen in midair, and looked up as though she had not heard right.

那名办事员愣住了，拿着圆珠笔的手也不动了。她抬头看着我，好像没有听清楚我说什么似的。

But the job is more challenging than most run-of-the-mill careers and the rewards are more of a satisfaction rather than just money.

但这项工作比大部分普通工作都具有挑战性，而它通常带来的回报不是金钱，更多的是满足感。

我的
父亲
My Father

The first memory I have of him — of anything, really — is his strength. It was in the late afternoon in a house under construction near ours. The unfinished wood floor had large, terrifying holes whose yawning darkness I knew led to nowhere good. His powerful hands, then age 33, wrapped all the way around my tiny arms, then age 4, and easily swung me up to his shoulders to command all I surveyed.

The relationship between a son and his father changes over time. It may grow and flourish in mutual maturity. It may sour in resented dependence or independence. With many children living in single-parent homes today, it may not even exist.

But to a little boy right after World War II, a father seemed a god with strange strengths and uncanny powers enabling him to do and know things that no mortal could do or know. Amazing things, like putting a bicycle chain back on, just like that. Or building a hamster cage.Or guiding a jigsaw so it forms the letter F; I learned the alphabet that way in those pre-television days.

There were, of course, rules to learn. First came the handshake. None of those fishy little finger grips, but a good firm squeeze accompanied by an equally strong gaze into the other's eyes. "The first thing anyone knows about you is your handshake," he would say. And we'd practice it each night on his return from work, the serious toddler in the battered Cleveland Indian's cap running up to the giant father to shake hands again and again until it was firm enough.

As time passed, there were other rules to learn. "Always do your best." "Do it now." "Never lie!" And most importantly,"You can do whatever you have to do." By my teens, he wasn't telling me what to do anymore, which was scary and heady at the same time. He provided perspective, not telling me what was around the great corner of life but letting me know there was a lot more than just today and the next, which I hadn't thought of.

One day, I realize now, there was a change. I wasn't trying to please him so much as I was trying to impress him. I never asked him to come to my football games. He had a high pressure career, and it meant driving through most of Friday night. But for all the big games, when I looked over at the sideline, there was that familiar fedora. And by God, did the opposing team captain ever get a firm handshake and a gaze he would remember.

Then, a school fact contradicted something he said. Impossible that he could be wrong, but there it was in the book. These accumulated over time, along with personal experiences, to buttress my own developing sense of values. And I could tell we had each taken our own, perfectly normal paths.

I began to see, too, his blind spots, his prejudices and his weaknesses. I never threw these up at him. He hadn't to me, and, anyway, he seemed to need protection. I stopped asking his advice; the experiences he drew from no longer seemed relevant to the decisions

I had to make.

He volunteered advice for a while. But then, in more recent years, politics and issues gave way to talk of empty errands and, always, to ailments.

From his bed, he showed me the many sores and scars on his misshapen body and all the bottles for medicine. "Sometimes," he confided, "I would just like to lie down and go to sleep and not wake up."

After much thought and practice ("You can do whatever you have to do."), one night last winter, I sat down by his bed and remembered for an instant those terrifying dark holes in another house 35 years before. I told my father how much I loved him. I described all the things people were doing for him. But, I said, he kept eating poorly, hiding in his room and violating the doctor's orders. No amount of love could make someone else care about life, I said; it was a two-way street. He wasn't doing his best. The decision was his.

He said he knew how hard my words had been to say and how proud he was of me."I had the best teacher,"I said."You can do whatever you have to do."He smiled a little. And we shook hands, firmly, for the last time.

Several days later, at about 4 A.M., my mother heard Dad shuffling about their dark room. "I have some things I have to do," he said. He paid a bundle of bills. He composed for my mother a long list of legal and financial what-to-do's "in case of emergency." And he wrote me a note.

Then he walked back to his bed and laid himself down. He went to sleep, naturally. And he did not wake up.

我对他——实际上是对所有事的最初记忆，就是他的力量。那是一个下午的晚些时候，在一所靠近我家的正在修建的房子里，尚未完工的木地板上有一个个巨大可怕的洞，那些张着大口的黑洞在我看来是通向不祥之处的。时年33岁的爸爸用那强壮有力的双手一把握住我的小胳膊，当时我才4岁，然后轻而易举地把我甩上他的肩头，让我把一切都尽收眼底。

　　父子间的关系是随着岁月的流逝而变化的，它会在彼此成熟的过程中成长兴盛，也会在令人不快的依赖或独立的关系中产生不和。而今许多孩子生活在单亲家庭中，这种关系可能根本不存在。

　　然而，对于一个生活在二战刚刚结束时期的小男孩来说，父亲就像神，他拥有神奇的力量和神秘的能力，他无所不能，无所不知。那些奇妙的事儿有上自行车链条，或是建一个仓鼠笼子，或是教我玩拼图玩具，拼出个字母"F"来。在那个电视机还未诞生的年代，我便是通过这种方法学会了字母表的。

　　当然，还得学些做人的道理。首先是握手。这可不是指那种冷冰冰的手指相握，而是一种非常坚定有力的紧握，并同样坚定有力地注视对方的眼睛。老爸常说："人们认识你首先是通过同你握手。"每晚他下班回家时，我们便练习握手。年幼的我，戴着顶破克利夫兰印第安帽，一本正经地跌跌撞撞地跑向巨人般的父亲，开始我们的握手。一次又一次，直到握得坚定，有力。

　　随着时间的流逝，还有许多其他的道理要学。比如："始终尽力而为"，"从现在做起"，"永不撒谎"，以及最重要的一条："凡是你必须做的事你都能做到"。当我十几岁时，老爸不再叫我做这做那，这既令人害怕又令人兴奋。他教给我判断事物的方法。他不是告诉我，在人生的重大转折点上将发生些什么，而是让我明白，除了今天和明天，还有很长的路要走，这一点我是从未考虑过的。

有一天，事情发生了变化，这是我现在才意识到的。我不再那么迫切地想要取悦老爸，而是迫切地想要给他留下深刻的印象。我从未请他来看我的橄榄球赛。他工作压力很大，这意味着每个星期五要拼命干大半夜。但每次大型比赛，当我抬头环视看台时，那顶熟悉的软呢帽总在那儿。并且感谢上帝，对方队长总能得到一次让他铭记于心的握手——坚定而有力，伴以同样坚定的注视。

后来，在学校学到的一个事实否定了老爸说过的某些东西。他不可能会错的，可书上却是这样写的。诸如此类的事日积月累，加上我的个人阅历，支持了我逐渐成形的价值观。我可以这么说：我俩开始各走各的阳关道了。

与此同时，我还开始发现他对某些事的无知，他的偏见，他的弱点。我从未在他面前提起这些，他也从未在我面前说起，而且，不管怎么说，他看起来需要保护了。我不再向他征求意见；他的那些经验也似乎同我要做出的决定不再相干。

老爸当了一段时间的"自愿顾问"，但后来，特别是近几年里，他谈话中的政治与国家大事让位给了空洞的使命与疾病。

躺在床上，他给我看他那被岁月扭曲了的躯体上的疤痕，以及他所有的药瓶儿。他倾诉着："有时我真想躺下睡一觉，永远不再醒来。"

通过深思熟虑与亲身体验（"凡是你必须做的事你都能做到"），去年冬天的一个夜晚，我坐在老爸床边，忽然想起35年前那另一栋房子里可怕的黑洞。我告诉老爸我有多爱他。我向他讲述了人们为他所做的一切。而我又说，他总是吃得太少，躲在房间里，还不听医生的劝告。我说，再多的爱也不能使一个人自己去热爱生命：这是一条双行道，而他并没有尽力，一切都取决于他自己。

他说他明白要我说出这些话多不容易，他是多么为我自豪。"我有位最好的老师，"我说，"凡是你必须做的事你都能做到"。他微微一笑，之后我们握手，那是一次坚定的握手，也是最后的一次。

几天后，大约凌晨4点，母亲听到父亲拖着脚步在他们漆黑的房间里走来走去。他说："有些事我必须得做。"他支付了一叠账单，给母亲留了张长长的条子，上面列有法律及经济上该做的事，"以防不测"。接着他留了封短信给我。

然后，他走回自己的床边，躺下。他睡了，十分安详，再也没有醒来。

yawning *adj.*
张着大嘴的
swung *v.*
摇摆
flourish *adj.*
繁茂
maturity *n.*
成熟
uncanny *adj.*
离奇的
hamster *n.*
仓鼠
jigsaw *n.*
拼板玩具
alphabet *n.*
字母表
fishy *adj.*
冷冰冰的
battered *adj.*
敲碎了的
heady *adj.*
使人兴奋的
confided *v.*
倾诉
shuffling *v.*
拖着

To a little boy right after World War II, a father seemed a god with strange strengths and uncanny powers enabling him to do and know things that no mortal could do or know.

对于一个生活在二战刚刚结束时期的小男孩来说，父亲就像神，他拥有神奇的力量和神秘的能力，他无所不能，无所不知。

In more recent years, politics and issues gave way to talk of empty errands and, always, to ailments.

近几年里，他谈话中的政治与国家大事让位给了空洞的使命与疾病。

She had been shopping with her Mom in Wal-Mart. She must have been 6 years old, this beautiful brown haired, freckle-faced image of innocence. It was pouring outside. The kind of rain that gushes over the top of rain gutters, so much in a hurry to hit the earth it has no time to flow down the spout.

We all stood there under the awning and just inside the door of the Wal-Mart. We waited, some patiently, others irritated because nature messed up their hurried day. I am always mesmerized by rainfall. I get lost in the sound and sight of the heavens washing away the dirt and dust of the world. Memories of running, splashing so carefree as a child come pouring in as a welcome reprieve from the worries of my day.

Her voice was so sweet as it broke the hypnotic trance we were all caught in. "Mom, let's run through the rain," she said.

"What?" Mom asked.

"Let's run through the rain!" She repeated.

"No, honey. We'll wait until it slows down a bit," Mom replied.

冒雨狂奔

Run Through the Rain

This young child waited about another minute and repeated: "Mom, let's run through the rain."

"We'll get soaked if we do," Mom said.

"No, we won't, Mom. That's not what you said this morning," the young girl said as she tugged at her Mom's arm."

"This morning? When did I say we could run through the rain and not get wet?"

"Don't you remember? When you were talking to Daddy about his cancer, you said, 'If God can get us through this, he can get us through anything!'"

The entire crowd stopped dead silent. I swear you couldn't hear anything but the rain. We all stood silently. No one came or left in the next few minutes. Mom paused and thought for a moment about what she would say.

Now some would laugh it off and scold her for being silly. Some might even ignore what was said. But this was a moment of affirmation in a young child's life. Time when innocent trust can be nurtured so that it will bloom into faith. "Honey, you are absolutely right. Let's run through the rain. If get wet, well maybe we just needed washing," Mom said. Then off they ran.

We all stood watching, smiling and laughing as they darted past the cars and. They held their shopping bags over their heads just in case. They got soaked. But they were followed by a few who screamed and laughed like children all the way to their cars. And yes, I did. I ran. I got wet. I needed washing. Circumstances or people can take away your material possessions, they can take away your money, and they can take away your health.

But no one can ever take away your precious memories. So, don't forget to make time and take the opportunities to make memories every day!

To everything there is a season and a time to every purpose under heaven. I hope you still take the time to run through the rain.

她和妈妈刚在沃尔玛购完物。这个天真的小女孩应该6岁大了，头发是美丽的棕色，脸上有雀斑。外面下着倾盆大雨，雨水溢满了檐槽，迫不及待地涌向大地，来不及排走。

我们都站在沃尔玛门口的遮篷下。大家在等待，有的人很耐心，也有人烦躁，因为老天在给他们本已忙碌的一天添乱。雨天总引起我的遐思。我出神地听着、看着老天洗刷冲走这世界的污垢和尘埃，孩时无忧无虑地在雨中奔跑玩水的记忆汹涌而至，暂时缓解了我这一天的焦虑。

小女孩甜美的声音打破了这令人昏昏欲睡的气氛，"妈妈，我们在雨里跑吧，"她说。

"什么？"母亲问。

"我们在雨里跑吧，"她重复。

"不，亲爱的，我们等雨小一点再走，"母亲回答说。

过了一会儿小女孩又说："妈妈，我们跑出去吧。"

"这样的话我们会湿透的，"母亲说。

"不会的，妈妈。你今天早上不是这样说的。"小女孩一边说一边拉着母亲的手。

"今天早上？我什么时候说过我们淋雨不会湿啊？"

"你不记得了吗？你和爸爸谈他的癌症时，你不是说'如果上帝让我们闯过这一关，那我们就没有什么过不去了。'"

人群一片寂静。我发誓，除了雨声，你什么都听不到。我们都静静地站着。接下来的几分钟没有一个人走动。母亲停了一下，在想着应该说些什么。

有人也许会对此一笑了之，或者责备这孩子的不懂事，有人甚至不把她的话放在心上。但这却是一个小孩子一生中需要被肯定的时候。若受到鼓舞，此时孩子单纯的信任就会发展成为坚定的信念。"亲爱的，你说得对，我们跑过去吧。如果淋湿了，那也许是因为我们的确需要冲洗一下了，"母亲说。然后她们就冲出去了。

我们站在那里，笑着看她们飞快地跑过停着的汽车。他们把购物袋高举过头想挡挡雨，但还是湿透了。好几个人像孩子般尖叫着，大笑着，也跟着冲了出去，奔向自己的车子。当然，我也这样做了，跑了出去，淋湿了。我也需要接受洗礼。环境或其他人可以夺去你的物质财富，抢走你的金钱，带走你的健康，但没有人可以带走你珍贵的回忆。因此，记得要抓紧时间，抓住机会每天都给自己留下一些回忆吧！

世间万物皆有自己的季节，做任何事情也有一个恰当的时机。希望你有机会在雨中狂奔一回。

freckle-faced *adj.*
满脸斑点的
innocence *n.*
无辜
mess *n.*
混乱
carefree *adj.*
无忧无虑的
hypnotic *adj.*
催眠的
trance *n.*
恍惚
tug *v.*
用力拖
 swear *v.*
发誓
affirmation *n.*
主张，肯定
scream *n.*
尖叫

The entire crowd stopped dead silent. I swear you couldn't hear anything but the rain.

人群一片寂静。我发誓，除了雨声，你什么都听不到。

To everything there is a season and a time to every purpose under heaven. I hope you still take the time to run through the rain.

世间万物皆有自己的季节，做任何事情也有一个恰当的时机。希望你有机会在雨中狂奔一回。

别停下，继续弹
Don't Stop

Wishing to encourage her young son's progress on the piano, a mother took her boy to a Paderewski concert. After they were seated, the mother spotted a friend in the audience and walked down the aisle to greet her.

Seizing the opportunity to explore the wonders of the concert hall, the little boy rose and eventually explored his way through a door marked "NO ADMITTANCE." When the house lights dimmed and the concert was about to begin, the mother returned to her seat and discovered that the child was missing.

Suddenly, the curtains parted and spotlights focused on the impressive Steinway on stage. In horror, the mother sawher little boy sitting at the key-board, innocently picking out Twinkle, Twinkle Little Star.

At that moment, the great piano master made his entrance, quickly moved to the piano, and whispered in the boy's ear, "Don't quit. Keep playing."

Then leaning over, Paderewski reached down with his lefthand and began filling in a bass part. Soon his right arm reached around to the other side of the child and he added a running obbligato. Together, the old master and the young novice transformed a frightening

190

situation into a wonderfully creative experience. The audience was mesmerized.

That's the way it is in life. What we can accomplish on our own is hardly noteworthy. We try our best, but the results aren't exactly graceful flowing music. But when we trust in the hands of a Greater Power, our life's work truly can be beautiful.

Next time you set out to accomplish great feats, listen carefully. You can hear the voice of the master, whispering in your ear, "Don't quit. Keep playing."

为了让儿子能在钢琴方面有长足的进步，一位母亲带着儿子去听帕德瑞夫斯基的音乐会。待她们坐定之后，那位母亲看到一位熟人，就穿过走道过去跟朋友打招呼。

小男孩好不容易有机会欣赏音乐厅的宏伟，他站了起来，并慢慢地摸索到了一扇门旁边，上面写着"禁止入内"。大厅里的灯暗了下来，音乐会马上就要开始了。那位母亲回到座位，却发现自己的孩子不见了。

这时候，幕布徐徐拉开，大厅里的聚光灯都集中到了舞台上的士坦威钢琴上。而让母亲吃惊的是，她的儿子竟然坐在钢琴面前，自顾自地弹着《闪烁，闪烁，小星星》。

这时候，著名的钢琴大师走上台，迅速地走到钢琴旁边，并在男孩的耳边轻声说道："孩子，别停下，继续弹。"

帕德瑞夫斯基俯下身去，用左手在键盘上弹奏低音部分。然后，他的右手绕过男孩的身后，弹奏出优美的伴奏。这位年长的钢琴大师和年幼的初学者一起，将原本紧张的气氛变成了一种全新的体验。全场的观众都听得入迷了。

其实，生活也是如此。我们所取得的成就不一定要多么显著。我们尽力了，结果却不一定能演奏出优美流畅的音乐。但是，如果我们相信大师的力量，我们的生活就会变的非常美丽。

当你准备伟大作品的时候，仔细地侧耳倾听，你会听到大师的声音在你耳边轻声说道："别停下，继续弹！"

seize v.
抓住
dim v.
变暗
bass n.
男低音
novice n.
初学者
mesmerize v.
施催眠术
noteworthy adj.
显著的
feat n.
技艺

Seizing the opportunity to explore the wonders of the concert hall, the little boy rose and eventually explored his way through a door marked "NO ADMITTANCE."

小男孩好不容易有机会欣赏音乐厅的宏伟，他站了起来，并慢慢地摸索到了一扇门旁边，上面写着"禁止入内"。

What we can accomplish on our own is hardly noteworthy. We try our best, but the results aren't exactly graceful flowing music.

我们所取得的成就不一定要多么显著。我们尽力了，结果却不一定能演奏出优美流畅的音乐。

家，甜蜜的家
Home, Sweet Home

（1）

Mid pleasures and palaces though we may roam,
虽然我们也会沉迷于欢乐与奢靡中，

Be it ever so humble, there's no place like home!
无论家是多么简陋，没有地方比得上它！

A charm from the skies seems to hallow us there,
好似从空而降的魔力，使我们感觉家的圣洁，

Which seek through the world, is ne'er met with elsewhere,
就是找遍全世界，也找不到像这样的地方，

Home! Home! Sweet, sweet Home!
家啊！家啊！甜蜜的家啊！

There's no place like Home! There's no place like Home!
没有地方比得上家！没有地方比得上家！

（2）
I gaze on the moon as I tread the drear wild,
每当我漫步荒野凝视明月，

And feel that my mother now thinks of her child,
便想起母亲正惦念着她的孩子，

As she looks on that moon from our own cottage door,
当她从茅舍门口遥望明月时，

Through the woodbine，whose fragrance shall cheer me no more.
穿过忍冬树丛，浓郁树香再也不能安慰我的心灵。

Home! Home! Sweet, sweet Home!
家啊！家啊！甜蜜的家啊！

There's no place like Home! There's no place like Home!
没有地方比得上家！没有地方比得上家！

（3）
An exile from home, splendor dazzles in vain;
对离乡背井的游子，再华丽的光辉，也是徒然闪烁；

Oh，give me my lowly thatch'd cottage again!
一栋矮檐茅舍！

The birds singing gaily, that came at my call—
一呼即来的鸟儿正在欢唱

Give me them, and the peace of mind, dearer than all!
赐给我它们——还有心灵的平静，这些胜过一切！

Home! Home! Sweet, sweet Home!
家啊！家啊！甜蜜的家啊！

There's no place like Home! There's no place like Home!
没有地方比得上家！没有地方比得上家！

roam v.
漫步
humble adj.
卑微的
hallow v.
视为神圣
tread v.
(以某种方式)行走
cottage n.
小屋，村舍
fragrance n.
芳香
splendor n.
光彩，壮观
dazzle v.
耀眼
gaily adj.
开心的

Be it ever so humble, there's no place like home!
无论家是多么简陋，没有地方比得上它！

名人眼中的母亲

Mother in Their Eyes

All that I am or ever hope to be, I owe to my angel Mother. I remember my mother's prayers and they have always followed me. They have clung to me all my life.

— Abraham Lincoln（1809~1865）

无论我现在怎么样，还是希望以后会怎么样，都应当归功于我天使一般的母亲。我记得母亲的那些祷告，它们一直伴随着我，而且已经陪伴了我一生。

——亚伯拉罕· 林肯(1809～1865)

My mother was the most beautiful woman I ever saw. All I am I owe to my mother. I attribute all my success in life to the moral, intellectual and physical education I received from her.

— George Washington(1732~1799)

我的母亲是我见过的最漂亮的女人。我所有的一切都归功于我的母亲。我一生中所有的成就都归功于我从她那儿得到的德、智、体的教育。

——乔治·华盛顿(1732～1799)

There never was a woman like her. She was gentle as a dove and brave as a lioness... The memory of my mother and her teachings were, after all, the only capital I had to start life with, and on that capital I have made my way.

— Andrew Jackson（1767~1845）

从来没有一个女人像她那样。她非常温柔，就像一只鸽子；她也很勇敢，就像一头母狮……毕竟，对母亲的记忆和她的教诲是我人生起步的惟一资本，并奠定了我的人生之路。

——安德鲁·杰克逊(1767～1845)

A good mother is worth a hundred schoolmaster.

— George Herbert（1593~1633）

一位好母亲抵得上一百个教师。

——乔治·赫伯特(1593～1633)

Youth fades; love droops; the leaves of friendship fall. A mother's secret hope outlives them all.

— Oliver Wendell Holmes（1809~1894）

青春会逝去；爱情会枯萎；友谊的绿叶也会凋零。而一个母亲内心的希望比它们都要长久。

——奥利弗·温戴尔·荷马(1809～1894)

God could not be everywhere and therefore he made mothers.

—Jewish proverb

上帝不能无处不在，因此他创造了母亲。

——犹太谚语

The heart of a mother is a deep abyss at the bottom of which you will always find forgiveness.

—Balzac（1799~1850）

母亲的心是一个深渊，在它的最深处你总会得到宽恕。

——巴尔扎克(1799～1850)

In all my efforts to learn to read, my mother shared fully my ambition and sympathized with me and aided me in every way she could. If I have done anything in life worth attention, I feel sure that I inherited the disposition from my mother.

— Booker T. Washington（1881~1915）

在我努力学习阅读的过程中，母亲一直分享着我的抱负、充分理解我，尽她所能帮助我。如果我一生中做了什么值得人们注意的事情，那一定是因为我继承了她的气质。

——布克·T·华盛顿(1881～1915)

It seems to me that my mother was the most splendid woman I ever knew... I have met a lot of people knocking around the world since, but I have never met a more thoroughly refined woman than my mother. If I have amounted to anything, it will be due to her.

— Charles Chaplin（1889~1977）

对我而言，我的母亲似乎是我认识的最了不起的女人……我遇见太多太多的世人，可是从未遇上像我母亲那般优雅的女人。如果我有所成就的话，这要归功于她。

——查尔斯·卓别林(1889～1977)

prayer *n.*
祈祷者
attribute to
归因于
lioness *n.*
母狮子
capital *n.*
资本
schoolmaster *n.*
教师
outlive *v.*
比…活得长
sympathize *v.*
同情
splendid *adj.*
辉煌的

The memory of my mother and her teachings were, after all, the only capital I had to start life with, and on that capital I have made my way.

毕竟，对母亲的记忆和她的教诲是我人生起步的惟一资本，并奠定了我的人生之路。

It seems to me that my mother was the most splendid woman I ever knew.

对我而言，我的母亲似乎是我认识的最了不起的女人。

无条件的母爱

Unconditional Mother's Love

I was a rotten teenager. Not a common spoiled, know-it-all, not-going-to-clean-my room, and self-conscious teenager. No, I was sharp-tongued and eager to control others. I told lies. And I realized at an early age that I could make things go my way with just a few small changes. The writers for today's hottest soap opera could not have created a worse character than me.

For the most part, and on the outside, I was a good kid, a giggly tomboy who liked to play sports and who was good at competition. This is probably why most people forgave me for my bad behavior towards people I felt to be of value.

Since I was clever enough to get some people to give in to me, I don't know how long it took me to realize how I was hurting so many others. Not only did I succeed in pushing away many of my closest friends by trying to control them; I also managed to destroy, time and time again, the most precious relationship in my life: my relationship with my mother.

Even today, almost 10 years since the birth of the new me, my former behavior astonishes me each time I reach into my memories. Hurtful words that cut and stung the

people I cared most about. Acts of confusion and anger that seemed to rule my every move — all to make sure that things went my way.

My mother, who gave birth to me at age 38 against her doctor's wishes, would cry to me, "I waited so long for you, please don't push me away. I want to help you!"

I would reply sharply, "I didn't ask for you! I never wanted you to care about me! Leave me alone and forget I ever lived!"

My mother began to believe I really meant it. My actions proved that.

I was mean and eager to control, trying to get my way at any cost. Like many young girls in high school, the boys whom I knew were impossible were always the first ones I had to date. I would get out of the house without my mother's knowing very late at night just to prove I could do it. I would readily tell complex lies without hesitation. I would also try to find any way to draw attention to myself while at the same time trying to be invisible.

I had been heavy into drugs during that period of my life, taking mind — changing pills and smoking things that changed my personality. That accounted for the terrible, sharp words that came flying from my mouth. However, that was not the case. My only addiction was hatred; my only pleasure was to make people feel pain.

But then I asked myself why. Why the need to hurt? And why the people I cared about the most? Why the need for all the lies? Why the attacks on my mother? I would drive myself mad with all the whys until one day, I couldn't stand it any longer and jump from a car moving at 80 miles per hour.

Lying awake the following night at the hospital, I came to realize that I didn't want to die.

And I did not want to inflict any more pain on people to cover up what I was truly trying to hide myself: self-hatred. Self-hatred inflicted on everyone else.

I saw my mother's pained face for the first time in years — warm, tired brown eyes filled with nothing but thanks for her daughter's rebirth of life and love for the child she waited 38 years to bear.

My first experience with unconditional love. What a powerful feeling.

Despite all the lies I had told her, she still loved me. I cried on her lap for hours one afternoon and asked why she still loved me after all the horrible things I did to her. She just looked down at me, brushed the hair out of my face and said frankly, "I don't know."

A kind of smile came out of her tears as the lines in her tested face told me all that I needed to know. I was her daughter, but more important, she was my mother. Not every rotten child is so lucky. Not every mother can be pushed to the limits time and time again, and come back with feelings of love.

Unconditional love is the most precious gift we can give. Being forgiven for the past is the most precious gift we can receive. I dare not say we could experience this pure love twice in one lifetime.

I was one of the lucky ones. I know that. I want to extend the gift my mother gave me to all the "rotten teenagers" in the world who are confused.

It's okay to feel pain, to need help, to feel love — just feel it without hiding. Come out from under the hard and protective covers, and take a breath of life.

我曾是个堕落的小丫头，不是一般的被宠坏，自以为是、不愿意打扫房间且自我意识强的那种。不，我不是那样的，我说话刻薄，控制别人的欲望强，又说谎。很早我就知道只要做些小小的变通，就可以随心所欲地操纵局面。就是现在最热门的肥皂剧作家也没能力塑造出比我更坏的角色。

多数时候，从表面上看，我是个好孩子，一个嘻嘻哈哈的假小子，喜欢体育运动，比赛常拿名次。或许正因为如此，尽管我对那些有身份的人任性胡来，他们中大多数人还是原谅了我。

我很精明，总有办法令别人让着我，所以我不知道我用了多长时间才意识到我伤害了这么多人。我不仅得罪了很多要好的朋友，因为我总试图摆布他们；而且我还一次又一次地践踏了我生活中最珍贵的亲情：母女之情。

即使在我重获新生10年之后的今天，每当我回忆往事，我还是对从前的所作所为深感震惊：我总是用刻薄的话伤害和刺痛我所关爱的人，我总用迷茫的举动和愤怒的情绪左右我的行为——而我这么做只是为了顺着性子。

我的母亲是在38岁的时候不顾医生的警告生下我的，她总是哭着对我说，"我等了这么长时间才得到你，求你不要推开我，我想帮你。"

而我总会尖刻地回答说，"我没叫你这么做，我从没有想过要你关心我！让我一个人呆着，就当我死了吧！"

我母亲开始相信我是来真的，因为我的行为证明了这一点。

我很自私，总想支配别人，不惜一切手段只是为了我行我素。像许多高中女生那样，我首先约会的总是那些高不可攀的男生。我常常晚上很晚时瞒着母亲溜出去，仅仅想证明我能得手。我会毫不犹豫地编造出有眉有眼的谎话来，我会想方设法吸引别人的注意力，同时又设法摆出一副低姿态。

在我生命的那段时间里，我沉湎于毒品之中，吸毒改变了我的心灵和人格，正因为如此我脱口而出的话总是那么可怕、尖刻。然而，我迷恋的不是毒品，我所迷恋的仅仅是仇恨，我唯一的快感就是使别人痛苦。

然后，我开始问自己：为什么会这样，有什么必要伤害别人？为什么受伤的恰是我最关心的人？为什么要撒谎？为什么要伤害我的母亲？所有这些"为什么"让我发疯，直到有一天我再也受不了了，从一辆时速80英里的车上跳了下来。

第二天晚上，我躺在医院里无法入眠，我意识到我不想死。

我并不想给别人制造更多的痛苦来掩饰我想逃避的东西——那就是自我仇视，一种给别人带来痛苦的自我仇视。

多年来，我第一次看清了母亲痛苦的面孔，她温暖、疲惫的棕色眼睛中充满了对女儿新生的感激和对她等了38年才怀上的女儿的爱。

我第一次体验到无条件的母爱，这是一种多么强烈的感情啊！

尽管我对她撒了那么多的谎，她依然爱我。一天下午，我躺在她膝盖上哭了几个小时，我问她为什么我做了那么多的蠢事，她却依然爱着我？她低头望着我，拂去我脸上的头发，诚恳地说："我不知道。"

慈祥的笑容透过眼泪从她的眼中流露出来，她那饱经岁月风霜的脸上的皱纹说明了一切。我是她的女儿，但更重要的是，她是我母亲。不是每一个堕落的孩子都像我这样幸运，不是每一个母亲都像我母亲那样一次次被逼上绝路却又一次次带着爱回到我身边。

无条件的爱是我们能够给予的最珍贵的礼物，过去的罪过得到原谅是我们能够得到的最宝贵的礼物。我敢说我们不可能在一生中两度体验这样纯洁的爱。

我以前多么地幸运呀！现在总算明白了。我想把从母亲那儿得到的礼物转送给世上所有迷茫、彷徨的失足青少年。

觉得痛苦、需要帮助、体验真爱，这些都是正常的，敞开心扉去迎接这一切吧。从坚硬的自我的外壳中解放出来，去呼吸生命的空气吧。

rotten *adj.*
腐烂的
sharp-tongued *adj.*
尖酸刻薄的
giggly *adv.*
傻笑的
tomboy *n.*
假小子
precious *adj.*
珍贵的
confusion *n.*
混乱
prove *v.*
证明
personality *n.*
人格
hatred *n.*
憎恨
attack *v.*
袭击
horrible *adj.*
可怕的

206

I realized at an early age that I could make things go my way with just a few small changes.

很早我就知道只要做些小小的变通，就可以随心所欲地操纵局面。

Unconditional love is the most precious gift we can give. Being forgiven for the past is the most precious gift we can receive.

无条件的爱是我们能够给予的最珍贵的礼物，过去的罪过得到原谅是我们能够得到的最宝贵的礼物。

天 使
The Angel

Once upon a time there was a child ready to be born. So one day he asked God, "They tell me you are sending me to earth tomorrow but how am I going to live there being so small and helpless?"

God replied, "Among the many angels, I chose one for you. She will be waiting for you and will take care of you."

But the child wasn't sure he really wanted to go. "But tell me, here in Heaven, I don't do anything else but sing and smile, that's enough for me to be happy."

"Your angel will sing for you and will also smile for you every day. And you will feel your angel's love and be happy."

"And how am I going to be able to understand when people talk to me," the child continued, "if I don't know the language that men talk?"

God patted him on the head and said, "Your angel will tell you the most beautiful and sweet words you will ever hear, and with much patience and care, your angel will teach you how to speak."

"And what am I going to do when I want to talk to you?"

But God had an answer for that question too. "Your angel will place your hands together and will teach you how to pray."

"I've heard that on earth there are bad men, who will protect me?"

"Your angel will defend you even if it means risking her life!"

"But I will always be sad because I will not see you anymore," the child continued warily.

God smiled on the young one. "Your angel will always talk to you about me and will teach you the way for you to come back to me, even though I will always be next to you."

At that moment there was much peace in Heaven, but voices from earth could already be heard. The child knew he had to start on his journey very soon. He asked God one more question, softly, "Oh God, if I am about to leave now, please tell me my angel's name."

God touched the child on the shoulder and answered, "Your angel's name is not hard to remember. You will simply call her Mommy."

　　从前，有个孩子马上就要诞生了。因此有一天他问上帝："听说明天你就送我去人间了，但是，我这么弱小和无助，我在那儿怎么生活呢？"

上帝答道："在众多的天使中，我特别为你挑了一位。她会守候你、无微不至地照顾你。"

小孩还是拿不准自己是否真的想去："但是在天堂，我除了唱唱笑笑外，什么也不做。这就足以让我感到幸福了。"

"你的天使每天会为你唱歌，为你微笑。你会感受她的爱，并且因此而幸福。"

"如果我不懂人类的语言，他们对我说话时，我怎么听得懂呢？"孩子继续问道。

上帝轻轻地拍了一下孩子的脑袋说："你的天使会对你说最美丽、最动听的话语，而这些都是你从未听过的。她会不厌其烦地教你说话。"

"如果我想与你说话怎么办？"

上帝胸有成竹地回答："你的天使会将你的双手合拢，教你如何祈祷。"

"听说尘世有很多坏蛋，谁来保护我呢？"

"即使冒着生命危险，你的天使也会保护你的。"

"但是见不到你，我会难过的。"小孩小心翼翼说道。

听到这儿，上帝对着小孩笑了。
"尽管我会一直陪伴你左右，你的天使
仍会提起我，教你重返天堂之路。"

此时，天堂一片宁静，凡间的声
音已可听到，小孩明白自己得赶紧上
路了。 他又轻声问了最后一个问题，
"哦，上帝，假如我现在就出发，请你
告诉我，我的天使叫什么名字。"

上帝把手放在小孩的肩上，答道：
"你的天使的名字很容易记住， 你就叫
她——妈妈。"

reply v.
回答
heaven n.
天堂
pat v.
轻拍
patience n.
耐心
risk v.
冒险

Your angel will tell you the most beautiful and sweet words you will ever hear, and with much patience and care, your angel will teach you how to speak.

你的天使会对你说最美丽、最动听的话语，而这些都是你从未听过的。她会不厌其烦地教你说话。

Your angel will always talk to you about me and will teach you the way for you to come back to me, even though I will always be next to you.

尽管我会一直陪伴你左右，你的天使仍会提起我，教你重返天堂之路。

母亲的教诲

What Mother Taught Me

My mother taught me to appreciate a job well done:

"If you're going to kill each other, do it outside. I just finished cleaning!"

My mother taught me religion:

"You'd better pray that will come out of the carpet."

My mother taught me about time travel:

"If you don't straighten up, I'm going to knock you into the middle of next week!"

My mother taught me logic:

"Because I said so, that's why!"

My mother taught me foresight:

"Be sure you wear clean underwear in case you're in an accident."

My mother taught me about contortion:

"Will you look at the dirt on the back of your neck!"

My mother taught me about stamina:

"You'll sit there 'til all that spinach is finished."

My mother taught me about weather:

"It looks as if a tornado swept through your room."

My mother taught me how to solve physics problems:

"If I yelled because I saw a meteor coming toward you, would you listen then?"

My mother taught me about hypocrisy:

"If I've told you once, I've told you a million times. Don't exaggerate!!!"

My mother taught me about envy:

"There are millions of less fortunate children in this world who don't have wonderful parents like you do!"

我母亲教我如何珍惜他人辛苦劳动：

"如果你们要打架，到外边打去——我刚整理好房间！"

我母亲教我什么是宗教：

"你最好祈祷那个东西能从地毯下冒出来。"

我母亲教我什么是时间旅行：

"你要是不改，我把你一把推到下周三！"（意为：不让过周末。）

我母亲教我什么是逻辑：

"为什么？因为我就是这么说的！"

我母亲教我什么是远见：

"一定要穿干净内衣，以防万一你遇到事故。"

我母亲教我什么是柔体杂技：

"你能不能看看你脖子后面的泥！"

我母亲教我什么是耐力：

"坐在那儿，直到把所有的菠菜吃完。"

我母亲教我认识天气：

"好像有龙卷风席卷过你的房间。"

我母亲教我如何解决物理学问题：

"如果我高声叫喊，是因为我看见有一颗流星正朝你俯冲而来，那你会不会听我的话？"

我母亲教我什么是伪善：

"如果我曾告诉过你一次，我实际上已告诉过你一百万次——不许夸张！！！"

我母亲教我什么是嫉妒：

"这世界上有数百万不幸的孩子，他们可没有你这么好的父母。"

appreciate v.	
欣赏，赞赏	
pray v.	
祈祷	
foresight v.	
远见	
stamina n.	
毅力	
meteor n.	
流星	
hypocrisy n.	
伪善	
fortunate adj.	
幸运的	

If I yelled because I saw a meteor coming toward you, would you listen then?

如果我高声叫喊，是因为我看见有一颗流星正朝你俯冲而来，那你会不会听我的话？

There are millions of less fortunate children in this world who don't have wonderful parents like you do!

这世界上有数百万不幸的孩子，他们可没有你这么好的父母。

母性的真谛

What Motherhood Really Means

Time is running out for my friend. While we are sitting at lunch she casually mentions she and her husband are thinking of starting a family. "We're taking a survey," she says, half-joking. " Do you think I should have a baby?"

" It will change your life," I say, carefully keeping my tone neutral. " I know," she says, " no more sleeping in on weekends, no more spontaneous holidays ..."

But that's not what I mean at all. I look at my friend, trying to decide what to tell her. I want her to know what she will never learn in childbirth classes. I want to tell her that the physical wounds of child bearing will heal, but becoming a mother will leave her with an emotional wound so raw that she will be vulnerable forever.

I consider warning her that she will never again read a newspaper without thinking: "What if that had been MY child?" That every plane crash, every house fire will haunt her. That when she sees pictures of starving children, she will wonder if anything could be worse than watching your child die. I look at her carefully manicured nails and stylish suit and think that no matter how sophisticated she is, becoming a mother will reduce her to the primitive level of a bear protecting her cub.

I feel I should warn her that no matter how many years she has invested in her career, she will be professionally derailed by motherhood. She might arrange for child care, but one day she will be going into an important business meeting, and she will think her baby's sweet smell. She will have to use every ounce of discipline to keep from running home, just to make sure her child is all right.

I want my friend to know that every decision will no longer be routine. That a five-year-old boy's desire to go to the men's room rather than the women's at a restaurant will become a major dilemma. The issues of independence and gender identity will be weighed against the prospect that a child molester may be lurking in the lavatory. However decisive she may be at the office, she will second—guess herself constantly as a mother.

Looking at my attractive friend, I want to assure her that eventually she will shed the added weight of pregnancy, but she will never feel the same about herself. That her own life, now so important, will be of less value to her once she has a child. She would give it up in a moment to save her offspring, but will also bcgin to hopc for morc ycars —not to accomplish her own dreams — but to watch her children accomplish theirs.

I want to describe to my friend the exhilaration of seeing your child learn to hit a ball. I want to capture for her the belly laugh of a baby who is touching the soft fur of a dog for the first time. I want her to taste the joy that is so real it hurts.

My friend's look makes me realize that tears have formed in my eyes. "You'll never regret it," I say finally. Then, squeezing my friend's hand, I offer a prayer for her and me and all of the mere mortal women who stumble their way into this holiest of callings.

时光任苒，朋友已经老大不小了。我们坐在一起吃饭的时候，她漫不经心地提到她和她的丈夫正考虑要小孩。"我们正在做一项调查，"她半开玩笑地说，"你觉得我应该要个小孩吗？"

"他将改变你的生活。"我小心翼翼地说道，尽量使语气保持客观。"这我知道。"她答道，"周末睡不成懒觉，再也不能随心所欲休假了……"

但我说的绝非这些。我注视着朋友，试图整理一下自己的思绪。我想让她知道她永远不可能在分娩课上学到的东西。我想让她知道：分娩的有形伤疤可以愈合，但是做母亲的情感伤痕却永远如新，她会因此变得十分脆弱。

我想告诫她：做了母亲后，每当她看报纸时就会情不自禁地联想："如果那件事情发生在我的孩子身上将会怎样啊！"每一次飞机失事、每一场住宅火灾都会让她提心吊胆。看到那些忍饥挨饿的孩子们的照片时，她会思索：世界上还有什么比眼睁睁地看着自己的孩子饿死更惨的事情呢？我打量着她精修细剪的指甲和时尚前卫的衣服，心里想到：不管她打扮多么考究，做了母亲后，她会变得像护崽的母熊那样原始而不修边幅。

我觉得自己应该提醒她，不管她在工作上投入了多少年，一旦做了母亲，工作就会脱离常规。她自然可以安排他人照顾孩子，但说不定哪天她要去参加一个非常重要的商务会议，却忍不住想起宝宝身上散发的甜甜乳香。她不得不拼命克制自己，才不至于为了看看孩子是否安然无恙而中途回家。

我想告诉朋友，有了孩子后，她将再也不能按照惯例做出决定。在餐馆，5岁的儿子想进男厕而不愿进女厕将成为摆在她眼前的一大难题：她将在两个选择之间权衡一番：尊重孩子的独立和性别意识，还是让他进男厕所冒险被潜在的儿童性骚扰者侵害？任凭她在办公室多么果断，作为母亲，她仍经常事后后悔自己当时的决定。

注视着我的这位漂亮的朋友，我想让她明确地知道，她最终会恢复到怀孕前的体重，但是她对自己的感觉已然不同。她现在视为如此重要的生命将随着孩子的诞生而变得不那么宝贵。为了救自己的孩子，她时刻愿意献出自己的生命。但她也开始希望多活一些年头，不是为了实现自己的梦想，而是为了看着孩子们美梦成真。

我想向朋友形容自己看到孩子学会击球时的喜悦之情。我想让她留意宝宝第一次触摸狗的绒毛时的捧腹大笑。我想让她品尝快乐，尽管这快乐真实得令人心痛。

朋友的表情让我意识到自己已经是热泪盈眶。"你永远不会后悔，"我最后说。然后紧紧地握住朋友的手，为她、为自己、也为每一位艰难跋涉、准备响应母亲职业神圣的召唤的平凡女性献上自己的祈祷。

survey *n.*
调查
half-joking *adj.*
半开玩笑的
childbirth *n.*
分娩
wound *n.*
伤
spontaneous *adj.*
自发的
neutral *adj.*
中立的
cub *n.*
幼兽
sophisticated *adj.*
复杂的
primitive *adj.*
基本的

discipline *n.*

训练，纪律

lurk *v.*

潜伏

lavatory *n.*

厕所

pregnancy *n.*

怀孕

offspring *n.*

后代

exhilaration *n.*

愉快

capture *v.*

捕获

stumble *v.*

绊跌，绊脚

I look at her carefully manicured nails and stylish suit and think that no matter how sophisticated she is, becoming a mother will reduce her to the primitive level of a bear protecting her cub.

我打量着她精修细剪的指甲和时尚前卫的衣服，心里想到：不管她打扮多么考究，做了母亲后，她会变得像护崽的母熊那样原始而不修边幅。

Then, squeezing my friend's hand, I offer a prayer for her and me and all of the mere mortal women who stumble their way into this holiest of callings.

然后紧紧地握住朋友的手，为她、为自己、也为每一位艰难跋涉、准备响应母亲职业神圣的召唤的平凡女性献上自己的祈祷。

欣赏篇

美 丽

Beauty

It is not, of course, the desire to be beautiful that is wrong but the obligation to be — or to try. What is accepted by most women as a flattering idealization of their sex is a way of making women feel inferior to what they actually are — or normally grow to be. For the ideal of beauty is administered as a form of self-oppression. Women are taught to see their bodies in parts, and to evaluate each part separately. Breasts, feet, hips, waistline, neck, eyes, nose, complexion, hair, and so on-each in turn is submitted to an anxious, fretful, often despairing scrutiny. Even if some pass muster, some will always be found wanting. Nothing less than perfection will do.

In men, good looks are a whole, something taken in at a glance. It does not need to be confirmed by giving measurements of different regions of the body, nobody encourages a man to dissect his appearance, feature by feature. As for perfection, that is considered trivial almost unmanly. Indeed, in the ideally good-looking man a small imperfection or blemish if considered positively desirable. According to one movie critic (a woman) who is a declared Robert Redford fan, it is having that cluster of skin-colored moles on one check that saves Redford from being merely a "pretty face". Think of the depreciation of women — as well as of beauty-that is implied in that judgment.

当然渴望美丽的愿望并没有什么错，错在美丽——或者说费尽心机变得美丽——成了女人的义务。大多数妇女以为美丽是对她们性别理想化的恭维，实际上却使她们对自己本来的样子——或者说正常的长相——感到羞耻。因为对美丽理想的追求是通过自我压抑来实现的。女人学会了把自己的身体分成各个部分来看，对每部分进行单独评价。胸、足、臀部、腰围、脖子、眼睛、鼻子、肤色、头发——每个部分都受到焦虑不安地细细评审。即使某些部分通过检验，总还有一些部分达不到要求。达不到完美无缺便不算美丽。

对男人而言，长相好指的是整体，是瞟一眼就能得到的整体印象。不必对身体的不同部分进行测量，也没有人鼓励一个男子把他外表的各个部分分开来看。至于完美的外表，那是无关紧要的——几乎可以说不够男人味儿。实际上，理想的美男子有一点缺陷或瑕疵反倒令人向往。据一位自认是罗伯特·雷德福影迷的电影评论家（女性）所言，雷德福脸上那片近肤色的胎记使他免于沦为仅仅只有一张"漂亮的脸蛋"。想想隐含在这番话中对女性的贬损——也是对美丽的贬损。

obligation *n.*
义务，责任

flattering *adj.*
谄媚的，奉承的

idealization *n.*
理想化

inferior *adj.*
下等的

complexion *n.*
面色，肤色

scrutiny *n.*
详细审查

dissect *v.*
把……解剖，切开仔细研究

blemish *n.*
污点，瑕疵

depreciation *n.*
贬值，降价

It is not, of course, the desire to be beautiful that is wrong but the obligation to be — or to try.

当然渴望美丽的愿望并没有什么错，错在美丽——或者说费尽心机变得美丽——成了女人的义务。

Nothing less than perfection will do.

达不到完美无缺便不算美丽。

Indeed, in the ideally good-looking man a small imperfection or blemish if considered positively desirable.

实际上，理想的美男子有一点缺陷或瑕疵反倒令人向往。

爱生活

Love Your Life

However mean your life is, meet it and live it do not shun it and call it bad names. It is not so bad as you image. It looks poorest when you are richest. The fault-finder will find faults in paradise.

Love your life, poor as it is. You may perhaps have some pleasant, thrilling, glorious hours, even in a poorhouse. The setting sun is reflected from the windows of the alms-house as brightly as from the rich man's abode; the snow melts before its door as early in the spring. I do not see but a quiet mind may live as contentedly there, and have as cheering thoughts, as in a palace. The town's poor seem to me often to live the most independent lives of any. Maybe they are simply great enough to receive without misgiving. Most think that they are above being supported by the town; but it often happens that they are not above supporting themselves by dishonest means. Which should be more disreputable. Cultivate poverty like a garden herb, like sage. Do not trouble yourself much to get new things, whether clothes or friends,turn the old, return to them.

Things do not change; we change. Sell your clothes and keep your thoughts.

不论你的生活如何贫穷，你要面对它生活，不要躲避它，更别用恶言咒骂它。它不像你想像那样坏。你最富有的时候，倒是看似最穷。爱找缺点的人就是到天堂里也能找到缺点。

你要爱你的生活，尽管它贫穷。甚至在一个济贫院里，你也还有愉快、高兴、光荣的时候。夕阳反射在济贫院的窗上，像照在富户人家窗上一样光亮；在那门前，积雪同在早春融化。我只看到，一个从容的人，在哪里都像在皇宫中一样，生活得心满意足而富有愉快的思想。城镇中的穷人，我看，倒往往是过着最独立的生活。也许他们是足够贫困而受之不愧。大多数人以为他们是超然的，不靠城镇来支援他们；可是事实上他们是往往利用了不正当的手段来对付生活，他们是毫不超脱的，毋宁是不体面的。视贫穷如园中之花而像圣人一样耕植它吧！不要找新的花样，无论是新的朋友或新的衣服，来麻烦你自己。找旧的，回到那里去。

万物不变，是我们在变。你的衣服可以卖掉，但要保留你的思想。

shun *v.*

避开，避免

alms-house *n.*

济贫院；养老院

abode *n.*

住所，住处

disreputable *adj.*

声名狼藉的

The setting sun is reflected from the windows of the alms-house as brightly as from the rich man's abode;

夕阳反射在济贫院的窗上，像照在富户人家窗上一样光亮；

I do not see but a quiet mind may live as contentedly there, and have as cheering thoughts, as in a palace.

我只看到，一个从容的人，在哪里都像在皇宫中一样，生活得心满意足而富有愉快的思想。

Cultivate poverty like a garden herb, like sage.

视贫穷如园中之花而像圣人一样耕植它吧！

钓鱼者

All Fishermen

There was a group called "the Fisherman's Fellowship". They were surrounded by streams and lakes full of hungry fish. They met regularly to discuss the call to fish, and the thrill of catching fish. They got excited about fishing!

Someone suggested that they needed a philosophy of fishing, so they carefully defined and redefined fishing, and the purpose of fishing. They developed fishing strategies and tactics. Then they realized that they had been going at it backwards. They had approached fishing from the point of view of the fisherman, and not from the point of view of the fish. How do fish view the world? How does the fisherman appear to the fish? What do fish eat, and when? These are all good things to know. So they began research studies, and attended conferences on fishing. Some traveled to far away places to study different kinds of fish, with different habits. Some got PhD's in fishology. But no one had yet gone fishing.

So a committee was formed to send out fishermen. As prospective fishing places outnumbered fishermen, the committee needed to determine priorities.

A priority list of fishing places was posted on bulletin boards in all of the fellowship halls. But still, no one was fishing. A survey was launched, to find out why... Most did not answer the survey, but from those that did, it was discovered that some felt called to study fish, a few to furnish fishing equipment, and several to go around encouraging the fisherman.

What with meetings, conferences, and seminars, they just simply didn't have time to fish.

Now, Jake was a newcomer to the Fisherman's Fellowship. After one stirring meeting of the Fellowship, Jake went fishing. He tried a few things, got the hang of it, and caught a choice fish. At the next meeting, he told his story, and he was honored for his catch, and then scheduled to speak at all the Fellowship chapters and tell how he did it. Now, because of all the speaking invitations and his election to the board of directors of the Fisherman's Fellowship, Jake no longer has time to go fishing.

But soon he began to feel restless and empty. He longed to feel the tug on the line once again. So he cut the speaking, he resigned from the board, and he said to a friend, "Let's go fishing." They did, just the two of them, and they caught fish.

The members of the Fisherman's Fellowship were many, the fish were plentiful, but the fishers were few.

在一个河湖密布鱼虾成群的地方成立了一个"钓鱼者协会"，他们时常聚在一起畅谈钓鱼的心得和钓鱼所带来的种种欢乐，他们热衷于钓鱼。

一些人提出应该对钓鱼形成一套理论，因此，他们谨慎地对钓鱼和钓鱼的目的进行了反复的定义。他们提出了关于钓鱼的战略和战术。但很快他们又意识到这样去研究钓鱼其实是一个倒退，因为他们仍然是从渔夫的角度而不是从鱼本身的角度来探讨钓鱼这一行为的。世界在鱼的眼里究竟是怎么样的？渔夫的出现对鱼又意味着什么？鱼吃什么，何时进食？这些才是需要弄懂的问题，于是他们又开始了研究，参加关于钓鱼的讨论会，有些人还不辞千里到各地研究不同种类、不同习性的鱼。有些人成为了研究鱼类的博士，但是他们当中没有一个真正去钓过鱼。

考虑到可供钓鱼的地方多而钓鱼者少，协会为此还专门成立了一个委员会来评估各种钓鱼场所，并给这些场所先后排名。

于是，协会各个大厅的公告栏上都贴了一份名册表注明哪些地方可以优先钓鱼，但结果还是没有谁去钓。为什么会出现这样的现象呢？协会又发起了问卷调查，大部分人没有反应，但从那些填写了问卷的人可以得知，有些人是在忙着研究鱼类，有些是在忙着完善钓鱼的装备，还有一些正在忙着到处发动人们去钓鱼。

太多的聚会，太多的研讨会要开，他们根本就没有时间去钓鱼。

杰克是协会里的一名新人，在开完一次激动人心的会议后，他就跑去钓鱼了。在试过好多新方法之后，他掌握了其中的窍门，钓上了一条上等大鱼。在接下来的一次会议上，杰克讲述了经验，并以此为荣，跟着在协会的所有会议上，都要邀请杰克谈一番他是如何钓上那条鱼的。如今，因为要忙着去应付演讲，已成为协会董事的杰克再抽不出时间可以去钓鱼了。

很快的杰克开始觉得不安和空虚了，他渴望能再次体会到鱼上钩收线时的那种感觉，所以他决定不再演讲了并辞去了董事一职，他对一个朋友说："我们钓鱼去吧！"于是他们两个人就去钓鱼去了，而且还钓到了鱼。

钓鱼者协会的会员很多，水里的鱼也很多，但真正的钓鱼者却没有几个。

fellowship *n*.
伙伴关系
thrill *v*.
紧张，激动
tactic *n*.
策略
priority *n*.
优先权
outnumber *v*.
数量上超过
fishology *n*.
钓鱼理论，钓鱼学

He longed to feel the tug on the line once again.
他渴望能再次体会到鱼上钩收线时的那种感觉。

The members of the Fisherman's Fellowship were many, the fish were plentiful, but the fishers were few.
钓鱼者协会的会员很多，水里的鱼也很多，但真正的钓鱼者却没有几个。

闲言碎语 Gossip

A woman repeated a bit of gossip about a neighbor. Within a few days the whole community knew the story. The person it concerned was deeply hurt and offended. Later the woman responsible for spreading the rumor learned that it was completely untrue. She was very sorry and went to a wise old sage to find out what she could do to repair the damage.

"Go to the marketplace," he said, "and purchase a chicken, and have it killed. Then on your way home, pluck its feathers and drop them one by one along the road." Although surprised by this advice, the woman did what she was told.

The next day the wise man said, "Now go and collect all those feathers you dropped yesterday and bring them back to me."

The woman followed the same road, but to her dismay, the wind had blown the feathers all away. After searching for hours, she returned with only three in her hand.

"You see," said the old sage, "it's easy to drop them, but it's impossible to get them back. So it is with gossip. It doesn't take much to spread a rumor, but once you do, you can never completely undo the wrong."

一个妇女说了有关邻居的一点闲言碎语。几天内社区所有的人都知道了此事。

当事人深深地受到了伤害与冒犯。后来，对散布谣言应负责任的那位妇女认识到事情完全不符合事实。她非常难过，就去聪明的老贤者那儿去请教如何弥补这种伤害。

"去集市吧，"他说，"买一只鸡，把它杀了。然后在你回家的路上，拔下它的羽毛，一片片的沿路扔掉。"

尽管这位妇女对这个忠告感到很惊奇，还是按照被告知的方法做了。

第二天，贤者说："现在，你去把昨天扔掉的那些羽毛全部收集起来，把它们交给我。"

妇女沿同一条路走着，但使她失望的是大风已把所有的羽毛吹跑了。她寻找了几个小时后，回来了，手里只有三根羽毛。

"你明白了吧，"老贤者说，"扔掉它们是容易的事，但不可能把它们找回来了。流言蜚语也是这样。散布谣言并不费力，可是一旦你做了这种事，永远也不能彻底消除这种不义行为了。"

gossip *n.*
闲话
offend *v.*
冒犯
purchase *v.*
购买
feather *n.*
羽毛
rumor *n.*
流言
dismay *v.*
使沮丧
sage *n.*
贤者

It doesn't take much to spread a rumor, but once you do, you can never completely undo the wrong.

散布谣言并不费力，可是一旦你做了这种事，永远也不能彻底消除这种不义行为了。

假如我知道，这是最后一次

If I Knew it Would Be the Last Time

If I knew it would be the last time that I'd see you fall asleep,

I would tuck you in more tightly and pray the Lord, your soul to keep.

If I knew it would be the last time that I see you walk out the door,

I would give you a hug and kiss and call you back for just one more.

If I knew it would be the last time I'd hear your voice lifted up in praise,

I would video tape each action and word, so I could play them back day after day.

If I knew it would be the last time, I could spare an extra minute or two to stop and say "I love you,"

Instead of assuming you would know I do.

If I knew it would be the last time I would be there to share your day,

Well, I'm sure you'll have so many more, I can let just this one slip away.

For surely there's always tomorrow to make up for an oversight,

And we always get a second chance to make everything right.

There will always be another day to say our "I love you",

And certainly there's another chance to say our "Anything I can do for you?"

But just in case I might be wrong, and today is all I get,
I'd like to say how much I love you and I hope we never forget,

Tomorrow is not promised to anyone, young or old alike,
Today may be the last chance you get to hold your loved one tight.

So if you're waiting for tomorrow, why not do it today?
For if tomorrow never comes, you'll surely regret the day,

That you didn't take that extra time for a smile, a hug, or a kiss,
Too busy to grant someone what turned out to be their last wish.

So hold your loved ones close today, whisper in their ear,
Tell them how much you love them and that you'll always hold them dear.

Take time to say "I'm sorry," "Please forgive me," "Thank you" or "It's okay".
And if tomorrow never comes, you'll have no regrets about today.

　　假如我知道，这是最后一次看着你入睡，我要为你紧掖好被角，祈祷上帝把你灵魂守牢。

　　假如我知道，这是最后一次送你走出家门，我会叫你转回头，再给你一次吻和拥抱。

假如我知道，我会在感激中听你的声音响起，我会刻录下你的言语和动作，以便我能天天重温这个美好时刻。

假如我知道，我要挤出每一分一秒，停下来认真地对你说"我爱你"，不会再像平日里那样敷衍了事。

假如我知道，我会在那儿陪着你度过，我坚信好运会降临，我能让这厄运悄悄溜掉。

总以为会有明天，可以弥补犯下的过失，总以为会有第二次机会，能够把每件事情做得完美。总以为还有另一天，说"我爱你"；总以为还有另一次机会，说"能为你做点什么吗"。

事实上我错了，我只能拥有今天，我应该告诉你我是多么多么爱你，多么希望我们永不离弃。明天没有与任何人相约，无论你年轻还是年老，今天或许是最后的一次机会，和你心爱的人紧紧依偎。

为何还在等待明天，今天不赶紧去做？如果明天永不再来，你会悔恨这一天。

如果你无法抽出时间，给朋友一个问候，给爱人一个拥抱、亲吻或笑脸，也许这就成了他们最终的遗憾。

在今天紧拥着你爱的人吧，在他们耳边低语，告诉他们你是多么地爱他们，多么渴望和他们在一起。

抓紧时间说一声"对不起"吧，说"请原谅"、"谢谢你"或者"太好了"吧，如果明天不再来到，你也不会为今天的事后悔。

tuck *v.*

卷起，打褶

spare *v.*

拨出，腾出，让给

whisper *v.*

耳语，私语

If I knew it would be the last time, I could spare an extra minute or two to stop and say "I love you," Instead of assuming you would know I do.

假如我知道，我要挤出每一分一秒，停下来认真地对你说"我爱你"，不会再像平日里那样敷衍了事。

Life's Journey

生命的旅程

We convince ourselves that life will be better after we get married, have a baby. Then we are frustrated that the kids aren't old enough and we'll be more content when they are. After that, we're frustrated that we have teenagers to deal with. We will certainly be happy when they are out of that stage. We tell ourselves that our lives will be complete when our spouse gets his or her act together, when we get a nicer car, are able to go on a nice vacation, when we retire. The truth is, there's no better time to be happy than right now. If not now, when?

Your life will always be filled with challenges. It's best to admit this to yourself and decide to be happy anyway. One of my favorite quotes comes from Alfred D. Souza. He said, "For a long time it had seemed to me that life was about to begin — real life. But there was always some obstacle in the way, something to be gotten through first, some unfinished business, time still to be served, or a debt to be paid. Then life would begin. At last it dawned on me that these obstacles were my life".

This perspective has helped me to see that there is no way to happiness. Happiness is the way. So, treasure every moment that you have and remember that time waits for no one. So... stop waiting until you finish school, until you go back to school, until you lose ten pounds, until you gain ten pounds, until you have kids, until your kids leave the house, until you start work, until you retire, until you get married, until you get divorced, until Friday night, until Sunday morning, until you get a new car or home, until spring, until summer, until fall, until winter, until you die, or until you are born again to decide that there is no better time than right now to be happy.

Happiness is a journey, not a destination.

我们总是相信，等我们结了婚，生了孩子生活会更美好。等有了孩子，我们又因为他们不够大而烦恼，想等他们大些时，我们就会开心了。可等他们进入青少年时期，我们还是同样地苦恼，于是又相信等他们过了这一阶段，幸福就会到来。我们告诉自己，等夫妻间任一方肯于合作，等我们拥有更好的车，等我们能去度一次美妙的假期，等我们退休后，我们的生活一定会完美的。而事实的真相是，没有任何时刻比现在更宝贵。倘若不是现在，又会是何时？

生活每时每刻都会有挑战。最好是让自己接受这一事实，无论如何使自己保持快乐的心境。我很欣赏艾尔弗雷德·D·苏泽的一段名言。他说："长期以来，我都觉得生活——真正的生活似乎即将开始。可是总会遇到某种障碍，如得先完成一些事情：没做完的工作，要奉献的时间，该付的债，之后生活才会开始。最后我醒悟过来了，这些障碍本身就是我的生活。"

这一观点让我意识到没有什么通往幸福的道路。幸福本身就是路。所以，珍惜你拥有的每一刻，且记住时不我待，不要再作所谓的等待 ——等你上完学，等你再回到学校；等你丢失了十英镑；等你获得十英镑；等你有了孩子或孩子长大离开家；等你开始工作或等你退休；等你结婚；等你离婚；等到周五晚上；等到周日早晨；等你有了新车或新房；等春天来临；等夏天来临；等秋天来临；等冬天来临；等你死去，等你有幸再来世上走一遭才明白此时此刻最应快乐。

　　幸福是一个旅程，不是终点站。

frustrate *v.*

挫败（某人的计划或意图；阻止）

quote *n.*

引言

perspective *n.*

视角

destination *n.*

目的地

The truth is, there's no better time to be happy than right now.

而事实的真相是，没有任何时刻比现在更宝贵。

It's best to admit this to yourself and decide to be happy anyway.

最好是让自己接受这一事实，无论如何使自己保持快乐的心境。

Treasure every moment that you have and remember that time waits for no one.

珍惜你拥有的每一刻，且记住时不我待。